She smiled at him and shook her head. "You were so kind to me, so tender..."

Her cheeks heated as she held his gaze and remembered being naked in his arms. "I'm sure I gave you the wrong impression of me that night. It wasn't like me to...with a complete stranger." She bit her lower lip and felt tears well in her eyes again.

"There is nothing wrong with the impression you left with me. As a matter of fact, I've thought of you often." He smiled. It was a great smile. "Every time I heard one of those songs that we'd danced to that night—" his gaze warmed to a Caribbean blue "—I thought of you."

She looked away to swallow the lump that had formed in her throat before she could speak again. "It wasn't an old boyfriend I was running from that night. I let you believe that because I doubted you'd have believed the truth..."

COWBOY'S REDEMPTION

New York Times Bestselling Author
B.J. DANIELS

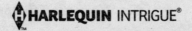
HARLEQUIN INTRIGUE®

This one is for Stelly, who even at four loves stories where the heroine gets to help save herself.

ISBN-13: 978-1-335-63913-4

Cowboy's Redemption

Copyright © 2018 by Barbara Heinlein

Recycling programs for this product may not exist in your area.

HARLEQUIN®
www.Harlequin.com

Printed in U.S.A.

B.J. Daniels is a *New York Times* and *USA TODAY* bestselling author. She wrote her first book after a career as an award-winning newspaper journalist and author of thirty-seven published short stories. She lives in Montana with her husband, Parker, and three springer spaniels. When not writing, she quilts, boats and plays tennis. Contact her at bjdaniels.com, on Facebook or on Twitter, @bjdanielsauthor.

Books by B.J. Daniels

Harlequin Intrigue

The Montana Cahills

Cowboy's Redemption

Whitehorse, Montana: The McGraw Kidnapping

Dark Horse
Dead Ringer
Rough Rider

HQN Books

A Cahill Ranch Novel

Renegade's Pride
Outlaw's Honor
Hero's Return

Visit the Author Profile page at Harlequin.com.

CAST OF CHARACTERS

Major Colt McCloud—The Montana cowboy is torn between the family ranch and his love for his job flying army helicopters—until a woman he spent a night with a year ago shows up at his door with a heartbreaking mission for him.

Lola Dayton—She always prided herself on her independence. But even she can't do this rescue alone—not when it involves finding out the truth about her baby daughter, Grace.

The Society of Lasting Serenity—Even some of the members are beginning to question leader Jonas Emanuel after the California cult moves to a mountaintop in Montana.

Jonas Emanuel—After seeing her photo and hearing her parents talk about Lola, the leader of the cult will do anything to have her. Even if it means keeping her prisoner on the Montana mountaintop complex. Even if it means using her baby daughter.

Sister Rebecca—She knows all of the leader's secrets, which is her mistake.

Sheriff Flint Cahill—His hands are tied when it comes to the religious cult. But he fears that Colt and Dayton aren't going to let anything stop them from finding out the truth about Baby Grace.

Lillie and Darby Cahill—Colt is lucky to have such good friends he can depend on.

Tommy Garrett—He knows better than anyone why Colt loves to fly choppers and he will do anything for his friend.

Chapter One

Running blindly through the darkness, Lola didn't see the tree limb until it struck her in the face. It clawed at her cheek, digging into a spot under her right eye as she flung it away with her arm. She had to stifle the cry of pain that rose in her throat for fear she would be heard. As she ran, she felt warm blood run down to the corner of her lips. The taste of it mingled with the salt of her tears, but she didn't slow, couldn't. She could hear them behind her.

She pushed harder, knowing that, being men, they had the advantage, especially the way she was dressed. Her long skirt caught on something. She heard the fabric rend, not for the first time. She felt as if it was her heart being ripped out with it.

Her only choice was to escape. But at what

price? She'd been forced to leave behind the one person who mattered most. Her thundering heart ached at the thought, but she knew that this was the only way. If she could get help...

"She's over here!" came a cry from behind her. "This way!"

She wiped away the warm blood as she crashed through the brush and trees. Her legs ached and she didn't know how much longer she could keep going. Fatigue was draining her. If they caught her this time...

She tripped on a tree root, stumbled and almost plunged headlong down the mountainside. Her shoulder slammed into a tree trunk. She veered off it like a pinball, but she kept pushing herself forward because the alternative was worse than death.

They were closer now. She could feel one of them breathing down her neck. She didn't dare look back. To look back would be to admit defeat. If she could just reach the road before they caught up to her...

Suddenly the trees opened up. She burst out of the darkness of the pines onto the blacktop of a narrow two-lane highway. The glare of headlights blinded her an instant before the shriek of rubber on the dark pavement filled the night air.

Chapter Two

Major Colt McCloud felt the big bird shake as he brought the helicopter low over the bleak landscape. He was back in Afghanistan behind the controls of a UH-60 Black Hawk. The throb of the rotating blades was drowned out by the sound of mortar fire. It grew louder and louder, taking on a consistent pounding that warned him something was very wrong.

He dragged himself awake, but the dream followed him. Blinking in the darkness, he didn't know where he was for a moment. Everything looked alien and surreal. As the dream began to fade, he recognized his bedroom at the ranch.

He'd left behind the sound of the chopper and the mortar fire, but the pounding had intensified. With a start, he realized what he was hearing.

Someone was at the door.

He glanced at the clock on his bedside table. It was after three in the morning. Throwing his legs over the side of the bed, he grabbed his jeans, pulling them on as he fought to put the dream behind him and hurry to the door.

A half dozen possibilities flashed in his mind as he moved quickly through the house. It still felt strange to be back here after years of traveling the world as an Army helicopter pilot. After his fiancée dumped him, he'd planned to make a career out of the military, but then his father had died, leaving him a working ranch that either had to be run or sold.

He'd taken a hundred-and-twenty-day leave in between assignments so he could come home to take care of the ranch. His father had been the one who'd loved ranching, not Colt. That's why there was a for-sale sign out on the road into the ranch.

Colt reached the front door and, frowning at the incessant knocking at this hour of the morning, threw it open.

He blinked at the disheveled woman standing there before she turned to motion to the driver of the car idling nearby. The engine roared and a car full of what appeared to be partying teenagers took off in a cloud of dust.

Colt flipped on the porch light as the woman turned back to him and he got his first good look at her and her scratched, blood-streaked face. For a moment he didn't recognize her, and then it all came back in a rush. Standing there was a woman he'd never thought he'd see again.

"Lola?" He couldn't even be sure that was her real name. But somehow it fit her, so maybe at least that part of her story had been true. "What happened to you?"

"I had nowhere else to go." Her words came out in a rush. "I was so worried that you wouldn't be here." She burst into tears and slumped as if physically exhausted.

He caught her, swung her up into his arms and carried her into the house, kicking the door closed behind him. His mind raced as he tried to imagine what could have happened to bring her to his door in Gilt Edge, Montana, in the middle of the night and in this condition.

"Sit here," he said as he carried her in and set her down in a kitchen chair before going for the first-aid kit. When he returned, he was momentarily taken aback by the memory of this woman the first time he'd met her. She wasn't beautiful in the classic sense. But she was striking, from her wide violet eyes fringed with pale lashes to the silk of her long blond hair. She had looked like an angel, especially in the long white dress she'd been wearing that night.

That was over a year ago and he hadn't seen her since. Nor had he expected to since they'd met initially several hundred miles from the ranch. But whatever had struck him about her hadn't faded. There was something flawless about her—even as scraped up and bruised as she was. It made him furious at whoever was responsible for this.

"Can you tell me what happened?" he asked as he began to clean the cuts.

"I... I..." Her throat seemed to close on a sob.

"It's okay, don't try to talk." He felt her trembling and could see that she was fighting tears. "This cut under your eye is deep."

She said nothing, looking as if it was all she could do to keep her eyes open. He took in her torn and filthy dress. It was long, like the white one he'd first seen her in, but faded. It reminded him of something his grandmother might have worn to do housework in. She was also thinner than he remembered.

As he gently cleaned her wounds, he could see dark circles under her eyes, and her long braided hair was in disarray with bits of twigs and leaves stuck in it.

The night he'd met her, her plaited hair had been pinned up at the nape of her neck—until he'd released it, the blond silk dropping to the center of her back.

He finished his doctoring, put away the first-aid kit, and wondered how far she'd come to find him and what she had been through to get here. When he returned to the kitchen, he found her standing at the back window, staring out. As she turned, he saw the fear in her eyes—and the exhaustion.

Colt desperately wanted to know what had happened to her and how she'd ended up on his doorstep. He hadn't even thought that she'd known his name. "Have you had anything to eat?"

"Not in the past forty-eight hours or so," she said, squinting at the clock on the wall as if not sure what day it was. "And not all that much before that."

He'd been meaning to get into Gilt Edge

and buy some groceries. "Sit and I'll see what I can scare up," he said as he opened the refrigerator. Seeing only one egg left, he said, "How do you feel about pancakes? I have chokecherry syrup."

She nodded and attempted a smile. She looked skittish as a newborn calf. Worse, he sensed that she was having second thoughts about coming here.

She licked her cracked lips. "I have to tell you. I have to explain—"

"It's okay. You're safe here." But safe from what, he wondered? "There's no hurry. Let's get you taken care of first." He'd feed her and get her settled down.

He motioned her into a chair at the kitchen table. He could tell that she must hurt all over by the way she moved. As much as he wanted to know what had happened, he thought she needed food more than anything else at this moment.

"While I make the pancakes, would you like a hot shower? The guest room is down the hall to the left. I can find you some clothes. They'll be too large for you, but maybe they will be more comfortable."

Tears welled in her eyes. He saw her swallow before she nodded. As she started to get to her feet, he noticed her grimace in pain.

"Wait."

She froze.

"I don't know how to say this delicately, but if someone assaulted you—"

"I wasn't raped."

He nodded, hoping that was true, because a shower would destroy important evidence. "Okay, so the injuries were…"

"From running for my life." With that she limped out of the kitchen.

He had the pancake batter made and the griddle heating when he heard the shower come on. He stopped to listen to the running water, remembering this woman in a hotel shower with him months ago.

That night he'd bumped into her coming out of the hotel bar. He'd seen that she was upset. She'd told him that she needed his help, that there was someone after her. She'd given him the impression she was running from an old boyfriend. He'd been happy to help. Now he wondered if that was still the case. She said she was running for her life—just as she had the first time they'd met.

But that had been in Billings. This was

Gilt Edge, Montana, hundreds of miles away. Didn't seem likely she would still be running from the same boyfriend. But whoever was chasing her, she'd come to him for help.

He couldn't turn her away any more than he'd been able to in that hotel hallway in Billings last year.

LOLA PULLED OUT her braid, discarding the debris stuck in it, then climbed into the steaming shower. She stood under the hot spray, leaned against the smooth, cool tile wall of the shower and closed her eyes. She felt weak from hunger, lack of sleep and constant fear. She couldn't remember the last time she'd slept through the night.

Exhaustion pulled at her. It took all of her energy to wash herself. Her body felt alien to her, her skin chafed from the rough fabric of the long dresses she'd been wearing for months. Stumbling from the shower, she wrapped her hair in one of the guest towels. It felt good to free her hair from the braid that had been wound at the nape of her neck.

As she pulled down another clean towel from the bathroom rack, she put it to her face and sniffed its freshness. Tears burned her eyes. It had been so long since she'd had even the smallest creature comforts like good soap, shampoo and clean towels that smelled like this, let alone unlimited hot water.

When she opened the bathroom door, she saw that Colt had left her a sweatshirt and sweatpants on the guest-room bed. She dried and tugged them on, pulling the drawstring tight around her waist. He was right, the clothes were too big, but they felt heavenly.

She took the towels back to the bathroom to hang them and considered her dirty clothing on the floor. The hem of the worn ankle-length coarse cotton dress was torn and filthy with dirt and grime. The long sleeves were just as bad except they were soiled with her blood. The black utilitarian shoes were scuffed, the heels worn unevenly since she'd inherited them well used.

She wadded up the dress and shoved it into the bathroom wastebasket before putting the shoes on top of it, all the time feeling as if she was committing a sin. Then again, she'd already done that, hadn't she.

Downstairs, she stepped into the kitchen to see Colt slip three more pancakes onto the stack he already had on the plate.

He turned as if sensing her in the doorway and she was reminded of the first time she'd seen him. All she'd noticed that night was his Army uniform—before he'd turned and she'd seen his face.

That he was handsome hadn't even registered. What she'd seen was a kind face. She'd been desperate and Colt McCloud had suddenly appeared as if it had been meant to be. Just as he'd been here tonight, she thought.

"Last time I saw you, you were on leave and talking about staying in the military," she said as he pulled out a kitchen chair for her and she sat down. "I was afraid that you had and that—" her voice broke as she met his gaze "—you wouldn't be here."

"I'm on leave now. My father died."

"I'm sorry."

He set down the plate of pancakes. "Dig in."

Always the gentleman, she thought as he joined her at the table. "I made a bunch. There's fresh sweet butter. If you don't like chokecherry syrup—"

"I love it." She slid several of the lightly browned cakes onto her plate. The aroma that rose from them made her stomach growl loudly. She slathered them with butter and covered them with syrup. The first bite was so delicious that she actually moaned, making him smile.

"I was going to ask how they are," he said with a laugh, "but I guess I don't have to."

She devoured the pancakes before helping herself to more. They ate in a companionable silence that didn't surprise her any more than Colt making her pancakes in the middle of the night or opening his door to her, no questions asked. It was as if it was something he did all the time. Maybe it was, she thought, remembering the first night they'd met.

He hadn't hesitated when she'd told him she needed his help. She'd looked into his blue eyes and known she could trust him. He'd been so sweet and caring that she'd almost told him the truth. But she'd stopped herself. Because she didn't think he would believe her? Or because she didn't want to involve him? Or because, at that point, she thought she could still handle things on her own?

Unfortunately, she no longer had the option of keeping the truth from him.

"I'm sure you have a lot of questions," she said, after swallowing her last bite of pancake and wiping her mouth with her napkin. The food had helped, but her body ached all over and fatigue had weakened her. "You had to be surprised to see me again, especially with me showing up at your door in the middle of the night looking like I do."

"I didn't even know you knew my last name."

"After that night in Billings… Before I left your hotel room, while you were still sleeping, I looked in your wallet."

"You planned to take my money?" He'd had over four hundred dollars in there. He'd been headed home to his fiancée, he'd told her. But the fiancée, who was supposed to pick him up at the airport, had called instead with crushing news. Not only was she not picking him up, she was in love with one of his best friends, someone he'd known since grade school.

He'd been thinking he just might rent a car and drive home to confront the two of them, he'd told Lola later. But, ultimately, he'd booked a flight for the next morning to where he was stationed and, with time to kill, had taken a taxi to a hotel, paid for a room and headed for the hotel bar. Two drinks later, he'd run into Lola as he'd headed from the bar to the men's room. Lola had saved him from getting stinking drunk that night. Also from driving to Gilt Edge to confront his ex-fiancée and his ex-friend.

"I hate to admit that I thought about taking your money," she said. "I could have used it."

"You should have taken it then."

She smiled at him and shook her head. "You were so kind to me, so tender..." Her cheeks heated as she held his gaze and remembered being naked in his arms. "I'm sure I gave you the wrong impression of me that night. It wasn't like me to...with a complete stranger." She bit her lower lip and felt tears well in her eyes again.

"There is nothing wrong with the impression you left with me. As a matter of fact, I've thought of you often." He smiled. It was a great smile. "Every time I heard one of those songs that we'd danced to in my hotel room that night—" his gaze warmed to a Caribbean blue "—I thought of you."

She looked away to swallow the lump that had formed in her throat before she could speak again. "It wasn't an old boyfriend I was running from that night. I let you believe that because I doubted you'd have believed the truth. I did need your help, though, because right before I collided with you in that hallway, I'd seen one of them in the hotel. I knew it was just a matter of time before they found me and took me back."

"Took you back?"

"I wasn't a fugitive from the law or some mental institution," she said quickly. "It's worse than that."

He narrowed his gaze with concern. "What could be worse than that?"

"The Society of Lasting Serenity."

Chapter Three

"The fringe religious cult that relocated to the mountains about five years ago?" Colt asked, unable to keep the shock from his voice.

She nodded.

He couldn't have been more stunned if she'd said she had escaped from prison. "When did you join that?"

"I didn't. My parents were some of the founding members when the group began in California. I was in Europe at university when they joined. I'd heard from my father that SLS had relocated to Montana. A few years after that, I received word that the leader, Jonas Emanuel, needed to see me. My mother was ill." Her voice broke. "Before I could get back here, my mother and father both died, within hours of each other, and had been buried on the compound. According to Jonas, they had one dying wish." Her laugh could have cut glass. "They wanted to see me married. Once I was on the SLS compound, I learned that, according to Jonas, they had promised me to him."

"That's crazy." He still couldn't get his head around this.

"Jonas is delusional but also dangerous."

"So you were running from him that night I met you?"

She nodded. "But, unfortunately, when I left the hotel the next morning, two of the 'sisters' were waiting for me and forced me to go back to the compound."

"And tonight?" he asked as he pushed his plate away.

Lola met his gaze. "I escaped. I'd been locked up there since I last saw you within miles of here at the Montana SLS compound."

Colt let out a curse. "You've been held there all this time against your will? Why didn't you—"

"Escape sooner?" She sounded near tears as she held his gaze.

He saw something in those beautiful eyes that made his stomach drop.

Her voice caught as she said, "I had originally gone there to get my parents' remains because I don't believe they died of natural causes. I'd gotten a letter from my father right before I heard from Jonas. He wanted out of SLS, but my mother refused. My father said he feared the hold Jonas had on her and needed my help because she wasn't well."

"What are you saying?"

"I think they were murdered, but I can't prove it without their bodies, and Jonas has refused to release them. Legally, there isn't much I can do since my parents had signed over everything to him—even their daughter."

Murder? He'd heard about the fifty-two-year-old charismatic leader of the cult living in the mountains outside of town, but he couldn't imagine the things Lola was telling him. "He can't expect you to marry him."

"Jonas was convinced that I would fall for him if I spent enough time at the compound, so he kept me there. At first, he told me it would take time to have my parents' remains exhumed and moved. Later I realized there was no way he was letting their remains go anywhere even if he could convince me to marry him, which was never going to happen."

Maybe it was the late hour, but he was having trouble making sense of this. "So after you met me…"

"I was more determined to free both my parents and myself from Jonas forever. I wasn't back at the compound long though, when I realized I was pregnant. Jonas realized it, too. I became a prisoner of SLS until the birth. Then Jonas had the baby taken away and had me locked up. I had to escape to get help for my daughter."

"Your daughter?"

She met his gaze. "That's why I'm here… She's *our* daughter," she said, her voice suddenly choked with tears. "Jonas took the baby girl that you and I made the first night we met."

COLT STARED AT HER, too shocked to speak for a moment. *What the hell?* "Are you trying to tell me—"

"I had your child but I couldn't contact you. Jonas kept me under guard, locked away. I had no way to get a message out. If any of the sisters tried to help me, they were severely punished."

He couldn't believe what he was hearing. "Wait. You had the baby at the compound?"

She nodded. "One of the members is a midwife. She delivered a healthy girl, but then Jonas had the child taken away almost at once. I got to hold her only for a few moments and only because Sister Amelia let me. She was harshly reprimanded for it. I got to look into her precious face. She has this adorable tiny heart-shaped birthmark on her left thigh and my blond hair. Just fuzz really." Tears filled her eyes again.

Colt ran a hand over his face before he looked at her again. "I'm having a hard time believing any of this."

"I know. If Jonas had let me leave with my daughter, I wouldn't have ever troubled you with any of this," she said.

"You would never have told me about the baby?" He hadn't meant to make it sound like an accusation. He'd expected her to be offended.

Instead, when she spoke, he saw only sympathy in her gaze. "When I met you, you were on leave and going back the next day. You were talking about staying in the Army. Your fiancée had just broken up with you."

"You don't have to remind me."

"What you and I shared that night..." She

met his gaze. "I'll never forget it, but I wasn't fool enough to think that it might lead to anything. The only reason I'm here now is that I need help to get our daughter away from that…man."

"Don't I have a right to know if I have a child?"

"Of course. But I wouldn't be asking anything of you—if Jonas hadn't taken our daughter. I'm more than capable of taking care of her and myself."

"What I don't understand is why Jonas wants to keep a baby that isn't his."

She didn't seem surprised by his skepticism, but when he looked into her eyes, he saw pain darken all that beautiful blue. "I can understand why you wouldn't believe she's yours."

"I didn't say that."

"You didn't have to." She got to her feet, grabbing the table to steady herself. "I shouldn't have come here, but I didn't know where else to go."

"Hold on," he said, pushing back his chair and coming around the table to take her shoulders in his hands. She felt small, fragile, and yet he saw a strength in her that belied her slim frame. "You have to admit this is quite the story."

"That's why I didn't tell you the night we met about the cult or the problems I was having getting my parents' remains out. I still thought I could handle it myself. Also I doubt you would have believed it." Her smile hurt him soul deep. "I wouldn't have believed it and I've lived through all of this."

He was doing his best to keep an open mind. He wasn't a man who jumped to quick conclusions. He took his time to make decisions based on the knowledge he was able to acquire. It had kept him alive all these years as an Army helicopter pilot.

"So what you're telling me is that the leader of SLS has taken your baby to force you to marry him? If he's so dangerous, why wouldn't he have just—"

"Forced me? He tried to…join with me, as he put it. He's still limping from the attempt. And equally determined that I will come to him. Now that I've shamed him…he will never let me have my baby unless I completely surrender to him in front of the whole congregation."

"Don't you mean *our* baby?"

Lola gave him an impatient look. Tears filled her eyes as she swayed a little as if having trouble staying upright after everything she'd been through.

He felt a stab of guilt. He'd been putting her through an interrogation when clearly she was exhausted. It was bad enough that she was scraped, cut and bruised, but he could see that her real injuries were more than skin deep.

"You're dead on your feet," he said. "There isn't anything we can do tonight. Get some rest. Tomorrow…"

A tear broke loose and cascaded down her cheek. He caught it with his thumb and gently wiped it away before she let him lead her to the guest bedroom where she'd showered earlier. His mind was racing. If any of this was true…

"Don't worry. We'll figure this out," Colt said as he pulled back the covers. "Just get some sleep." He knew he wouldn't be able to sleep a wink.

Could he really have a daughter? A daughter now being held by a crackpot cult leader? A man who, according to Lola, was much more dangerous than anyone knew?

Lola climbed into the bed, still wearing his

too-large sweats. He tucked her in, seeing that she could barely keep her eyes open.

"Dayton." At his puzzled look, she added, "That's my last name." They'd shared only first names the night they met. But that night neither of them had been themselves. She'd been running scared, and he'd been wallowing in self-pity over losing the woman he'd thought he was going to marry and live with the rest of his life.

"Lola Dayton," he repeated, and smiled down at her. "Pretty name."

He moved to the door and switched off the light.

"I named our daughter Grace," she said from out of the darkness. "Do you remember telling me that you always loved that name?"

He turned in the doorway to look back at her, too choked up to speak for a moment. "It was my grandmother's name."

LOLA THOUGHT SHE wouldn't be able to sleep. Her body felt leaden as she'd sunk under the covers. She could still feel the rough skin of Colt's thumb pad against her cheek and reached up to touch the spot. She hadn't been wrong about him. Not that first night. Not tonight.

She closed her eyes and felt herself careening off that mountain, running for her life, running for Grace's life. She was safe, she reminded herself. But Grace...

The sisters were taking good care of Grace, she told herself. Jonas wouldn't let anything happen to the baby. At least she prayed that he wouldn't hurt Grace to punish her even more.

The thought had her heart pounding until she realized the only power Jonas had over her was the baby. He wouldn't hurt Grace. He needed that child if he ever hoped to get what he wanted. And what he wanted was Lola. She'd seen it in his eyes. A voracious need that he thought only she could fill.

If he ever got his hands on her again... Well, she knew there would be no saving herself from him.

COLT KICKED OFF his boots and lay down on the bed fully dressed. Sleep was out of the question. If half of what Lola had told him was true... Was it possible they'd made a baby that night? They hadn't used protection. He hadn't had anything. Nor had she. It wasn't like him to take a chance like that.

But there was something so wholesome, so innocent, so guileless…

Rolling to his side, he closed his eyes. The memory was almost painful. The sweet scent of her body as she lay with her back to him naked on the bed. The warmth of his palm as he slowly ran it from her side down into the saddle of her slim waist to the rise of her hip and her perfectly rounded buttocks. The catch of her breath as he pulled her into him and cupped one full breast. The tender moan from her lips as he rolled her over to look into those violet eyes.

Groaning, Colt shifted to his back again to stare up at the dark ceiling. That night he'd lost himself in that delectable woman. He'd buried all feelings for his former fiancée into her. He'd found salvation in her body, in her arms, in her tentative touch, in her soft, sweet kisses.

He closed his eyes, again remembering the feel of her in his arms as they'd danced in his hotel room. The slow sway, their bodies joined, their movements more sensuous than even the act of love. He'd given her a little piece of his heart that night and had not even realized it.

Swinging his legs over the bed, he knew he'd never get any rest until he checked on her. Earlier, he'd gotten the feeling that she wanted to run—rather than tell him what had brought her to his door. She hadn't wanted to involve him, wouldn't have if Jonas didn't have her baby.

That much he believed. But why hadn't she told him what she was running from the night they'd first met? Maybe he could have helped her.

He moved quietly down the hallway, half-afraid he would open the bedroom door only to find her gone and all of this like his dream about being back in Afghanistan.

After easing open the door, he waited for his eyes to adjust to the blackness in the room. Her blond hair lay like a fan across her pillow. Her peaceful face made her appear angelic. He found himself smiling as he stared down at the sleeping Lola. He couldn't help wondering about their daughter. She would be three months old now. Did she resemble her mother? He hoped so.

The thought shook him because he realized how much he wanted to believe her. A daughter. He really could have a daughter? A baby

with Lola? He shook his head. What were the
chances that their union would bring a child
into this world? And yet he and Lola had done
more than make love that night. They'd connected in a way he and Julia never had.

The thought of Julia, though, made him re-
coil. Look how wrong he'd been about her.
How wrong he'd been about his own mother.
Could he trust his judgment when it came to
women? Doubtful.

He stepped out of the room, closing the door
softly behind him. Tomorrow, he told himself,
he would know the truth. He'd get the sheriff to go with them up to the compound and
settle this once and for all.

Colt walked out onto the porch to stare up
at the starry sky. The air was crisp and cold,
snow still capping the highest peaks around
town. He knew this all could be true. Normally, he would never have had intercourse
with a woman he didn't know without protection. But that night, he and Lola hadn't just
had sex. They'd made love, two lost souls
who'd given each other comfort in a world
that had hurt them.

He'd been heartbroken over Julia and his
friend Wyatt. Being in Lola's arms had saved

him. If their lovemaking had resulted in a baby...a little girl...

Yes, what was he going to do? Besides go up to that compound and get the baby for Lola? He tried to imagine himself as a father to an infant. What a joke. He couldn't have been in a worse place in his life to take on a wife and a child.

He looked across the ranch. All his life he'd felt tied down to this land. That his father had tried to chain him to it still infuriated him—and at the same time made him feel guilty. His father had had such a connection to the land, one that Colt had never felt. He'd loved being a cowboy, but ranching was more about trying to make a living off the land. He'd watched his father struggle for years. Why would the old man think he would want this? Why hadn't his father sold the place, done something fun with the money before he'd died?

Instead, he'd left it all to Colt—lock, stock and barrel, making the place feel like a noose around his neck.

"It's yours," the probate attorney had said. "Do whatever you want with the ranch."

"You mean I can sell it?"

"After three months. That's all your father

stipulated. That you live on the ranch for three months full-time, and then if you still don't want to ranch, you can liquidate all of your father's holdings."

Colt took a deep breath and let it out. "Sorry, Dad. If you think even three *years* on this land is going to change anything, you are dead wrong." He'd put in his three months and more waiting for an offer on the place.

When his leave was up, he was heading back to the Army and his real job. At least that had been the plan before he'd found Lola standing on his doorstep. Now he didn't know what to think. All he knew was that he had to fly. He didn't want to ranch. Once the place sold, there would be nothing holding him here.

He thought about Lola asleep back in the house. If this baby was his, he'd take responsibility, but he couldn't make any promises— not when he didn't even know where he would be living when he came home on leave.

Up by the road, he could see the for-sale sign by the gate into the ranch. With luck, the ranch would sell soon. In the meantime, he had to get Lola's baby back for her. His baby.

He pushed open the door and headed for his bedroom. Everything was going to work out.

Once Lola understood what he needed to do, what he had to do...

He lay down on the bed fully clothed again and closed his eyes, knowing there was no chance of sleep. But hours later, he woke with a start, surprised to find sunlight streaming in through the window. As he rose, still dressed, he worried that he would find Lola gone, just as she had been that morning in Billings.

The thought had his heart pounding as he padded down to the guest room. The door was partially ajar. What if none of it had been true? What if she'd realized he would see through all of it and had taken off?

He pressed his fingertips against the warm wood and pushed gently until he could see into the dim light of the room. She lay wrapped in one of his mother's quilts, her long blond hair splayed across the pillow. He eased the door closed, surprised how relieved he was. Maybe he wasn't a good judge of character when it came in women—Julia a case in point—but he wanted to believe Lola was different. It surprised him how *much* he wanted to believe it.

LOLA WOKE TO the smell of frying bacon. Her stomach growled. She sat up with a start, momentarily confused as to where she was. Not on the hard cot at the compound. Not locked in the claustrophobia-inducing tiny cabin with little heat. And certainly not waking to the wonderful scent of frying bacon at that awful prison.

Her memory of the events came back to her in a rush. What surprised her the most was that she'd slept. It had been so long that she hadn't been allowed to sleep through the night without being awakened as part of the brainwashing treatment. Or when the sisters had come to take her breast milk for the baby. She knew the only reason, other than exhaustion, she'd slept last night was knowing that she was safe. If Colt hadn't been there, though…

She refused to think about that as she got up. Her escape had cost her. She hurt all over. The scratches on her face and the sore muscles were painful. But far worse was the ache in her heart. She'd had to leave Grace behind.

Still dressed in the sweatshirt and sweatpants and barefoot, she followed the smell of frying bacon to the kitchen. Colt had music playing and was singing softly to a country music song. She had to smile, remembering how much he'd liked to dance.

That memory brought a rush of heat to her cheeks. She'd told herself that she hadn't been in her right mind that night, but seeing Colt again, she knew that was a lie. He'd liberated that woman from the darkness she'd been living in. He'd brought out a part of her she hadn't known existed.

He seemed to sense her in the doorway and turned, instantly smiling. "I hope you don't mind pancakes again. There was batter left over. I haven't been to the store. But I did find some bacon in the freezer."

"It's making my stomach growl. Is there anything I can do to help?"

"Nope, just bring your appetite." He motioned for her to take a seat. "I made a lot. I don't know about you, but I'm hungry."

She sat down at the table and watched him expertly flip pancakes and load up a plate with bacon.

As he set everything on the table and took a chair, he met her gaze. "How are you feeling?"

"Better. I slept well." For that he couldn't imagine how thankful she was. "On the compound, they would wake me every few hours to chant over me."

"Sounds like brainwashing," Colt said, his jaw tightening.

"Jonas calls it rehabilitation."

He pushed the bacon and pancakes toward her. "Eat while it's hot. We'll deal with everything else once we've eaten."

She looked into his handsome face, remembered being in his arms and felt a flood of guilt. If there was any other way of saving Grace, she wouldn't have involved him in this. But he had been involved since that night in Billings when she'd asked for his help and he hadn't hesitated. He just hadn't known then that what he was getting involved in was more than dangerous.

Once Jonas knew that Colt was the father of her baby... She shuddered at the thought of what she was about to do to this wonderful man.

Chapter Four

Colt picked at his food. He'd lied about being hungry. Just the smell of it turned his stomach. But he watched Lola wolf down hers as if she hadn't eaten in months. He suspected she hadn't eaten much. She was definitely thinner than she'd been that night in Billings a year ago.

But if anything, she was even more striking, with her pale skin and those incredible eyes. He was glad to see her hair down. It fell in a waterfall of gold down her back. He was reminded again how she'd looked the first time he'd seen her—and when he'd opened the door last night.

"I've been thinking about what we should do first," Colt said as he moved his food around the plate. "We need to start by getting you some clothing that fits," he said as if all they had to worry about was a shopping trip. "Then I think we should go by the sheriff's office."

"There is somewhere we have to go first," she said, looking up from cutting off a bite of pancake dripping with the red syrup. "I know you don't trust me. It's all right. I wouldn't trust me, either. But don't worry, you will." She smiled. She had a slight gap between her two front teeth that made her smile adorable. That and the innocence in her lightly freckled face had sucked him in from the first.

He'd been vulnerable that night. He'd been a broken man and Lola had been more than a temptation. The fact that she'd sworn he was saving her that night hadn't hurt, either.

He thought about the way she'd looked last night when he'd found her on his doorstep. She still had a scratch across one cheek and a cut under her right eye. It made her look like a tomboy.

"You have to admit, the story you told me last night was a little hard to believe."

"I know. That's why you have to let me prove it to you."

He eyed her suspiciously. "And how do you plan to do that?"

"Do you know a doctor in town who can examine me?"

His pulse jumped. "I thought you said—"

"Not for that. Or for my mental proficiency." Her gaze locked with his. "I need you to know that I had a baby three months ago. A doctor should be able to tell." He started to argue, but she stopped him. "This is where we need to start before we go to the sheriff."

He wanted to argue that this wasn't necessary, but they both knew it was. If a doctor said she'd never given birth and none of this was real, then it would be over. No harm done. Except the idea of him and Lola having a baby together would always linger, he realized.

"I used to go to a family doctor here in town. If he's still practicing..."

DR. HUBERT GRAY was a large man with a drooping gray mustache and matching bushy eyebrows over piercing blue eyes.

Colt explained what they wanted.

Dr. Gray narrowed his gaze for a moment, taking them both in. "Well, then, why don't you step into the examination room with my nurse, Sara. She'll get you ready while I visit with Colt here."

The moment Lola and Sara left the room, the doctor leaned back in his office chair. "Let me get this straight. You aren't even sure there is a child?"

"Lola says there is. Unfortunately, the baby isn't here."

The doctor nodded. "You realize this won't prove that the child is yours—just that she has given birth before."

Colt nodded. "I know this is unusual."

"Nothing surprises me. By the way, I was sorry to hear about your father. Damn cancer. Only thing that could stop him from ranching."

"Yes, he loved it."

"Tell me about flying helicopters. You know I have my pilot's license, but I've never flown a chopper."

Colt told him what he loved about it. "There is nothing like being able to hover in the air, being able to put it down in places—" he shook his head "—that seem impossible."

"I can tell that you love what you do, but did I hear you're ranching again?"

"Temporarily."

A buzz sounded and Dr. Gray rose. "This shouldn't take long. Sit tight."

True to his word, the doctor returned minutes later. Colt looked up expectantly. "Well?" he asked as Dr. Gray took his seat again behind his desk. Colt realized that his emotions were all over the place. He didn't know what he was hoping to hear.

Did he really want to believe that Lola had given birth to their child to have it stolen by some crazy cult leader? Wouldn't it be better if Lola had lied for whatever reason after becoming obsessed with him following their one-night stand?

"You wanted to know if she has recently given birth?" the doctor asked.

"Has she?" He held his breath, telling himself even if she had, it didn't mean that any of the rest of it was true.

"Since she gave me permission to provide you with this information, I'd say she gave birth in the past three months."

Just as she'd said. He glanced at the floor, not sure if he was relieved or not. He felt like a heel for having even a glimmer of doubt. But Lola was right. He'd had to know before he went any further with this. It wasn't like he really knew this woman. He'd simply shared one night of intimacy all those months ago.

There was a tap at the door. The nurse stuck her head in to say that the doctor had another patient waiting. Behind the nurse, he saw Lola in the hallway. She looked as if she'd been crying. He quickly rose. "Thank you, Doc," he said over his shoulder as he hurried to Lola, taking both of her hands in his. "I'm sorry. I'm so sorry. You didn't have to do this."

Her smile was sad but sweet as she shook her head. "I just got upset because Dr. Gray is so kind. I wish he'd delivered Grace instead of..." She shook her head. "Not that any of that matters now."

"It's time we went to the sheriff," he said as he led her out of the building. She seemed to hesitate, though, as they reached his pickup. "What?"

"Just that the sheriff isn't going to be able to do anything—and that's if he believes you."

"He'll believe me. I know him," he said as he opened the pickup door for her. "I went to school with his sister Lillie and her twin brother, Darby. Darby's a good friend. Both Lillie and Darby are new parents. As for the sheriff—Flint Cahill is as down-to-earth as anyone I know and I'm sure he's familiar with The Society of Lasting Serenity. Sheriff Cahill is also the only way we can get on church property—and off—without any trouble."

She still looked worried. "You don't know Jonas. He'll be furious that I went to the law. He'll also deny everything."

"We'll see about that." He went around the truck and slid behind the wheel. As he started the engine, he looked over at her and saw how anxious she was. "Lola, the man has taken our daughter, right?" She nodded. "Then I don't give a damn how furious he is, okay?"

"You don't know how he is."

"No, but I'm going to find out. Don't worry. I'm going to get to the bottom of this, one way or the other."

She looked scared, but said, "I trust you with my life. And Grace's."

Grace. Their child. He still couldn't imagine them having a baby together—let alone that some cult leader had her and refused to give her up to her own mother.

Common sense told him there had to be more to the story—and that's what worried him as he drove to the sheriff's department. Sheriff Cahill would sort it out, he told himself. As he'd said, he liked and trusted Flint.

Going up to the compound with the level-headed sheriff made the most sense.

Because if what Lola was telling him was true, they weren't leaving there without Grace.

SHERIFF FLINT CAHILL was a nice-looking man with thick dark hair and gray eyes. He ushered them right into his office, offered them a chair and something to drink. They took chairs, but declined a beverage.

"So what is this about?" the sheriff asked after they were all seated, the office door closed behind them.

Colt could see that Lola liked the sheriff from the moment she met him. There was something about him that exuded confidence, as well as honesty and integrity. She told him everything she had Colt. When she finished, though, Colt couldn't tell from Flint's expression what he was thinking.

The sheriff looked at him, his gray eyes narrowing. "I'm assuming you wouldn't have brought Ms. Dayton here if you didn't believe her story."

"I know this is unusual." He glanced over at her. Her scrapes and scratches were healing, and she looked good in the clothes they'd bought her. Still, he saw that she kept rubbing her hand on her thighs as if not believing she was back in denim.

At the store, he'd wanted to buy her more clothing, but she'd insisted she didn't need more than a couple pairs of jeans, two shirts, several undergarments and hiking shoes and socks. She'd promised to pay him back once she could get to her own money. Jonas had taken her purse with her cash and credit cards. Her money was in a California bank account. Once she had Grace, she said she would see about getting money wired up to her so she could pay him back.

Colt wasn't about to take her money, but he hadn't argued. The one thing he'd learned quickly about Lola was that she didn't expect or want anything from him—except help getting her baby from Jonas. That, she'd said, would be more than enough since it could get them both killed.

At the time, he'd thought she was exaggerating. Now he wasn't so sure.

"I believe her," Colt told the sheriff. "What do you know about The Society of Lasting Serenity?"

"Just that they were California based but

moved up here about five years ago. They keep to themselves. I believe their numbers have dropped some. Probably our Montana winters."

"You're having trouble believing that Jonas Emanuel would steal Lola's child," Colt said.

Flint sighed. "No offense but, yes, I am." He turned to Lola. "You say your only connection to the group was through your parents before their deaths and your return to the States?"

"Yes, they became involved after I left for college. I thought it was a passing phase, a sign of them not being able to accept their only child had left the nest."

"You never visited them at the California compound?" the sheriff asked.

"No, I got a teaching job right out of college in the Virgin Islands."

Flint frowned. "You didn't visit your parents before you left?"

Lola looked away. "By then we were…estranged. I didn't agree with some of the things they were being taught in what I felt was a fringe cult."

"So why would your parents promise you to Jonas Emanuel?" the sheriff asked.

She let out a bitter laugh. "To *save* me. My

mother believed that I needed Jonas's teaching. Otherwise, I was doomed to live a wasted life chasing foolish dreams and, of course, ending up with the wrong man."

"They wanted you to marry Jonas." Flint frowned. "Isn't he a little old for you?"

"He's fifty-two. I'm thirty-two. So it's not unheard-of."

The sheriff looked over at Colt, who was going to be thirty-three soon. Young for a major in the Army, he knew.

"I doubt my parents took age into consideration," Lola said. "One of the teachings at the SLS is that everyone is ageless. My parents, like the other members, were brainwashed."

"So you went to the compound after you were notified that your parents had died," the sheriff said.

"I questioned them both dying especially since earlier I'd received a letter from my father saying he wanted out but was having a hard time convincing my mother to leave SLS," she said. "Also I wanted to have them buried together in California, next to my older sister, who was stillborn. My parents were both in their forties when they had me. By then, they didn't believe they would ever conceive again."

"So you had their bodies—"

"Jonas refused to release them. He said they would be buried as they had wished—on the side of the mountain at the compound. I went up there determined to find out how it was that they had died within hours of each other. I also wanted to make him understand that I would get a lawyer if I had to—or go to the authorities."

"That's when you learned that you'd been promised to him?" the sheriff asked.

"Yes, as ridiculous as it sounds. When I refused, I was held there against my will until I managed to get away. I'd stolen aboard a van driven by two of the sisters, as they call them. That's when I met Colt."

"Why didn't you go to the police then?" Flint asked.

"I planned to the next morning. I'd gone into the back of the hotel when I saw one of the sisters coming in the front. I ducked down a hallway and literally collided with Colt. I asked for his help and he sneaked me up to his room."

The sheriff looked at Colt. "And the two of

you hit it off. She didn't tell you what she was running from?"

"No, but it was clear she was scared. I thought it was an old boyfriend."

Flint nodded and looked to Lola again. "You didn't trust him enough to ask for his help the next morning?"

"I didn't want to involve him. By then I knew what Jonas was capable of. This flock does whatever he tells them. The few who disobey are punished. One woman brought me extra food. I heard her being beaten the next morning by her own so-called sisters. When I had my daughter, they took her away almost at once. I could hear her crying, but I didn't get to see her again. The women would come in and take my breast milk, but they said she was now Jonas's child. He called her his angel. I knew I had only one choice. Escape and try to find Colt. I couldn't fight Jonas and his followers alone. And Jonas made it clear. The only way I could see my baby and be with her was if I married him and gave my life to The Society of Lasting Serenity."

Flint pushed back his chair and rose to his feet. "I think it's time I visited the compound and met this Jonas Emanuel."

Chapter Five

Colt followed the sheriff's SUV out of town toward the Judith Mountains. The mountains began just east of town and rose to the northeast for twenty miles. In most places they were only about ten miles wide with low peaks broken by stream drainages. But there were a number of peaks including the highest one, Judith Peak, at more than six thousand feet.

It was rugged country. Back in the 1950s the US Air Force had operated a radar station on top of the peak. The SLS had bought state land on an adjacent mountaintop in an isolated area with few roads in or out. Because it was considered a church, the SLS had rights that even the sheriff couldn't do anything about.

So Colt was nervous enough, but nothing compared to Lola. In the pickup seat next to him, he could feel her getting more agitated the closer they got to the SLS compound. He reached over to take her hand. It was ice-cold.

"It's going to be all right," he tried to assure her—and himself. If what she'd told him was true, then Jonas would have to hand over the baby. "Jonas will cooperate with a lawman."

She didn't look any more convinced than he felt. He'd dealt with religious fanatics for a while now and knew that nothing could stop them if they thought they were in the right.

"Jonas seems so nice, so truthful, so caring," she said. "He's fooled so many people. My parents weren't stupid. He caught them in his web with his talk of a better world." She shook her head. "But he is pure evil. I hate to even think what he might have done to my parents."

"You really think he killed them."

"Or convinced my mother to kill herself and my father."

Colt knew that wouldn't be a first when it came to cult mania.

"Clearly the sheriff wasn't called when they died. Jonas runs SLS like it's his own private country. He told me that his religious philosophy requires the bodies to be untouched and put into the ground quickly. Apparently in

Montana, a religious group can bury a body on their property without embalming if it is done within so many hours."

The road climbed higher up the mountain. Ahead, the sheriff slowed. Colt could see that an iron gate blocked them from going any farther. Flint stopped, put down his window and pushed a button on what appeared to be an intercom next to the gate. Colt whirred down his window. He heard a tinny-sounding voice tell him that someone would be right down to let them in.

A few minutes later, an older man drove up in a Jeep. He spoke for a few moments with the sheriff before opening the gate. As Colt drove through, he felt the man's steely gaze on him. Clearly the SLS didn't like visitors. The man who'd opened the gate was wearing a gun under his jacket. Colt had caught sight of the butt end of it when the man got out of his rig to open the gate.

As they passed, he noticed something else interesting. The man recognized Lola. Just the sight of her made the man nervous.

LOLA FELT HER BODY begin to vibrate inside. She thought she might throw up. The memories of being imprisoned here for so long made her itch. She fought the need to claw her skin, remembering the horrible feel of the cheap cloth dresses she was forced to wear, the taste of the tea the sisters forced down her throat, the horrible chanting that nearly drove her insane. That wasn't all they'd forced on her once they'd quit coming for her breast milk. There'd been the pills that Sister Rebecca had forced down her throat.

She felt a shiver and hugged herself against the memories, telling herself she was safe with Colt and the sheriff. But the closer they got to the compound, the more plagued she was with fear. She doubted either Colt or the sheriff knew who they were dealing with. Jonas had gotten this far in life by fooling people. He was an expert at it. At the thought of what lies he would tell, her blood ran cold even though the pickup cab felt unbearably hot.

"Are you all right?" Colt asked, sounding worried as he glanced over at her.

She nodded and felt a bead of perspiration run down between her shoulder blades. She wanted to scratch her arm, feeling as if something was crawling across it, but feared once she started she wouldn't be able to stop.

Just driving up here brought everything back, as if all the crazy they'd been feeding her might finally sink in and she'd be a zombie like the other "sisters." Isn't that what Jonas had hoped? Wasn't that why he was just waiting for her return? He knew she'd be back for Grace. She couldn't bear to think what he had planned for her.

By the time they reached the headquarters and main building of the SLS, there was a welcome group waiting for them. Lola recognized Sister Rebecca, the woman Jonas got to do most of his dirty work. Sister Amelia was there, as well, but she kept her head down as if unable to look at her.

Lola felt bad that she'd gotten the woman in trouble. She could still hear Amelia's cries from the beating she'd received for giving her extra food. She could well imagine what had happened to the guards after she'd escaped. Jonas would know that she hadn't been taking her pills with the tea. Sister Amelia would be blamed, but there had been nothing Lola could do about that.

Flint parked his patrol SUV in front of the main building. Colt parked next to him. Lola felt her body refuse to move as Colt opened his door. She stared at the two women standing like sentinels in front of them and fought to take her next breath.

"Would you feel better staying out here in the truck?" Colt asked.

She wiped perspiration from her lip with the back of her hand. How could she possibly explain what it was like being back here, knowing what they had done to her, what they might do again if Colt didn't believe her and help her?

Terrified of facing Jonas again, she thought of her baby girl and reached for her door handle.

COLT WONDERED IF bringing Lola back here wasn't a mistake. She looked terrified one moment and like a sleepwalker the next. What had they done to her? He couldn't even imagine, given what she'd told him about her treatment. They'd taken her baby, kept her locked up, hadn't let her sleep. He worried that was just the tip of the iceberg, though.

One of the two women, who were dressed in long simple white sheaths with their hair in braided buns, stepped forward to greet them.

"I'm Sister Rebecca. How may we help

you?" Appearing to be the older of the two, the woman's face had a blankness to it that some might have taken for serenity. But there was something else in the eyes. A wariness. A hardness.

"We're here to see Jonas Emanuel," the sheriff said.

"Let me see if he's available," she said, and turned to go back inside.

Colt started to say something about Jonas making himself available, but Flint stopped him. "Let's keep this as civilized as we can— at least to start."

The second woman stood at the foot of the porch steps, her fingers entwined and her face down, clearly standing guard.

A few moments later, Sister Rebecca came out again. "Brother Emanuel will see you now." She motioned them up the porch steps as the other woman drifted off toward a building in the pines where some women were washing clothes and hanging them on a string of clotheslines.

"Seems awfully cold to be hanging wash outside this time of year," Colt commented. Spring in Montana often meant the temperature never rose over forty in the mountains.

Sister Rebecca smiled as if amused. "We believe in hard work. It toughens a person up so a little cold weather doesn't bother us."

He thought about saying something about how she wasn't the one hanging clothes today in the cool weather on the mountaintop, but he followed the sheriff's lead and kept his mouth shut.

As Sister Rebecca led them toward the back of the huge building, Colt noticed the layout. In this communal living part of the structure, straight-backed wooden chairs were lined up like soldiers at long wooden tables. Behind the dining area, he could hear kitchen workers and the banging of pots and pans. An aroma arose that reminded him of school cafeterias.

What struck him was the lack of conversation coming from the kitchen, let alone any music. There was a utilitarian feeling about the building and everything in it—the workers included. They could have been robots for the lack of liveliness in the place.

Sister Rebecca tapped at a large wooden door. A cheerful voice on the other side said, "Come in." She opened the door and stood back to let them enter a room that was warm and cozy compared to the other part of the building.

A sandy-haired man, who Colt knew was fifty-two, had been sitting behind a large oak desk. But now he pushed back his office chair and rose, surprising Colt by not just his size, but how fit he was. He had boyish good looks, lively pale blue eyes and a wide, straight-toothed smile. He looked much younger than his age.

The leader came around his desk to shake hands with the sheriff and Colt. "Jonas Emanuel," he said. "Welcome." His gaze slid to Lola. When he spoke her name it was with obvious affection. "Lola," Jonas said, looking pained to see her scratched face before returning his gaze to Colt and the sheriff.

"We need to ask you a few questions," Sheriff Cahill said, introducing himself and Colt. "You already know Ms. Dayton."

"Please have a seat," Jonas said graciously, offering them one of the chairs circled around the warm blaze going in the rock fireplace to one side of the office area. Colt thought again of the women hanging wet clothes outside. "Can I get you anything to drink?"

They all declined. Jonas took a chair so he was facing them and crossed his legs to hold one knee in his hands. Colt noticed that he was limping before he sat down.

"How long have you known Ms. Dayton?" Flint asked.

"Her parents were founding members. Lola's been a member for the past couple of years," Jonas said.

"That's not true," she cried. "You know I'm not a member, would never be a member."

Colt could see that she was even more agitated than she'd been in the truck on the way up. She sat on the edge of her chair and looked ready to run again. "Just give me my baby," she said, her voice breaking. "I want to see my baby." She turned in her chair. Sister Rebecca stood at the door, fingers entwined, head down, standing sentry. "My baby. Tell her to get my baby."

Colt reached over and took her hand. Jonas noticed but said nothing.

"As you can see, Ms. Dayton is quite upset. She claims that you are holding her child here on the property," the sheriff said.

Jonas nodded without looking at Lola. "Perhaps we should speak in private. Lola? Why don't you go with Sister Rebecca? She can make you some tea."

"I don't want any of your so-called tea," Lola snapped. "I want my child."

"It's all right," Flint said. "Go ahead and leave with her. We need to talk to Jonas. We won't be long."

Lola looked as if she might argue, but when her gaze fell on Colt, he nodded, indicating that she should leave. "I'll be right here if you need me." Again he could feel Jonas's gaze on him.

After Sister Rebecca left with Lola, the leader sighed deeply. "I'm afraid Lola is a very troubled woman. I'm not sure what she's told you—"

"That you're keeping her baby from her," Colt said.

He nodded sadly. "Lola came to us after her parents died. She'd lost her teaching job, been fired. That loss and the loss of her parents... We tried to help her since she had no one else. I'm sure she's told you that her parents were important members of our community here. On her mother's death bed, she made me promise that I would look after Lola."

"She didn't promise Lola to you as your wife?" Colt asked, and got a disapproving look from the sheriff.

"Of course not." Jonas looked shocked by the accusation. "I had hoped Lola would stay with us. Her parents took so much peace in living among us, but Lola left."

"I understand she ran away some months ago," Flint said.

"A year ago," Colt added.

Again Jonas looked surprised. "Is that what she told you?" He shook his head. "I foolishly suggested that maybe time away from the compound would be good for her. Several of the sisters were making a trip to Billings for supplies. I talked Lola into going along. Once there, though, she apparently became turned around while shopping and got lost. In her state of mind, that was very traumatic. Fortunately, the sisters found her, but not until the next morning. She was confused and hysterical. They brought her back here where we nursed her back to health and discovered that while she'd been lost in Billings, she'd been assaulted."

Colt started to object, but the sheriff cut him off. "She was pregnant? Did she say who the father was?"

Jonas shook his head. "She didn't seem to

know." The man looked right at Colt, his blue eyes giving nothing away.

"Where is the baby now?" Flint asked.

"I'm afraid the infant was stillborn. A little boy. Which made it all the more traumatic and heartbreaking for her since we all knew that she had her heart set on having a baby girl. I'm not sure if you know this, but her mother had a daughter before Lola who was stillborn. I'm sure that could have played a part in what happened. When Lola was told that her own child had been stillborn, she had a complete breakdown and became convinced that we had stolen her daughter."

"Then you won't mind if we have a look around," the sheriff said.

"Not at all." He rose to his feet, and the sheriff and Colt followed. "I'm so glad Lola's been found. We've been taking care of her since her breakdown. Unfortunately, the other night she overpowered one of her sisters and, hysterical again, took off running into the woods. We looked for her for hours. I was going to call your office if we didn't hear from her by this afternoon. When she left, she forgot her pills. I was afraid she'd have another psychotic event with no one there to help her."

"Don't you mean when Lola *escaped* here?" Colt asked.

Jonas shook his head as if trying to be patient. "Escaped?" He chuckled. "Do you see razor wire fences around the compound? Why would she need to escape? We believe in free will here at Serenity. Lola can come and go as she pleases. She knows that. But when she's in one of her states…"

"What kind of medication is she on?" the sheriff asked.

"I have it right here," Jonas reached into his pocket. "I had Sister Rebecca bring it to me when I heard that you were at the gate. I was so glad that she had come back for it. I believe Dr. Reese said it's what they give patients with schizophrenia. I suppose she didn't mention to you that she'd been taking the medication. It helps with the anxiety attacks, as well as the hallucinations."

"Dr. Reese?" Flint asked.

"Ben Reese. He's our local physician, one of the best in the country and one of our members," Jonas said.

"I'd like to see where the baby was buried," Colt said.

"Of course. But let's start with the tour the sheriff requested."

Colt memorized the layout of the buildings as Jonas led them from building to building. Everywhere they went, there were people working, both men and women, but definitely there were more women on the compound than men. He saw no women with babies as most of the women were older.

"Our cemetery is just down here," Jonas said. Colt followed Jonas and the sheriff down a narrow dirt path that wound through the trees to open in a meadow. Wooden crosses marked the few graves, the names of the deceased printed on metal plaques.

He spotted a relatively fresh grave and felt his heart drop. It was a small plot of dark earth. What if Jonas was telling the truth? What if Lola had had a son? *His* son? And the infant was buried under that cold ground?

"It is always so difficult to lose a child," Jonas was saying. "We buried him next to Lola's parents. We thought that would give her comfort. If not now, later when she's…better. We're waiting for her to name him before we put up the cross."

"I think I've seen enough," Sheriff Cahill said, and looked at Colt.

Colt didn't know what to think. On the surface, it all seemed so…reasonable.

"Sister Rebecca took Lola to the kitchen," Jonas said. "Lunch will be ready soon. I believe we're having a nice vegetable soup today. You're welcome to join us. Some of the sisters are better cooks than others. I can attest that the ones cooking today are our best."

"Thank you, but I need to get back to Gilt Edge," Flint said. "What about you, Colt?"

He knew the sheriff wasn't asking just about lunch or returning to town. "I'll see what Lola wants to do," he said, after taking a last look at the small unmarked grave before heading back toward the main building.

"If Lola is determined not to stay with us, I just hope she'll get the help she needs," Colt heard Jonas tell the sheriff. "I'm worried about her, especially after your visit. Clearly she isn't herself."

LOLA SHOVED AWAY the cup of tea Sister Rebecca had tried to get her to drink. She'd seen Colt and the sheriff go out to search the complex with Jonas. "I know you hid her the moment the sheriff punched the intercom at the gate. Please…" Her voice broke. "I just want to see her so I know she's all right."

Sister Rebecca reached over to pat her hand—and shove the tea closer with her other hand.

Lola jerked her hand back. "You can't keep her. She's mine." Tears burned her eyes. "Keeping a baby from her mother…"

"You aren't taking your medication, are you? It makes you like this. You really should take it so you're more calm."

"Brain-dead, you mean. Half-comatose, so I'm easy to manipulate. If you keep me drugged up, I won't cause any trouble, right?"

"You wouldn't have left here if you'd been taking your medication." Sister Rebecca shook her head. "You know we were only trying to help you. I should have been the one giving you your medication instead of Sister Amelia. She let you get away with not taking it and look what's happened to you, you poor dear."

Lola scoffed. "As if you care. And Sister Amelia didn't know anything about what I was doing," she said quickly, fearing that the next beating Amelia got could kill her.

"I was hiding them under my tongue until she turned away."

The woman nodded. "Well, should you end up staying here, we won't let that happen again, will we."

"I'm not staying here."

Sister Rebecca said nothing as the front door opened and Colt came in. Through the open doorway, Lola could see Jonas and the sheriff standing out by the patrol SUV. She could tell that Jonas had convinced the sheriff that she was crazy.

Standing up too quickly, Lola knocked over her chair. It clattered to the floor. Dizzy, she had to hang on to the table for a moment. When the light-headedness passed and she could let go, she started for the door. But not before she realized Colt had seen her having trouble standing.

She swept past him, determined not to let the sheriff leave. Her baby was hidden somewhere in the complex. Jonas had had one of his followers hide her. The sheriff had to find her. Lola had to convince him—

At the sound of a baby crying, she stumbled to an abrupt stop. "Do you hear that?" she called down to the sheriff from the top of the porch steps. "It's my baby crying." He looked up in surprise. So did Jonas. Both seemed to stop to listen.

For a moment, Lola thought that she had imagined it. Fear curdled her stomach. She felt Colt's hand on her shoulder as he reached for her. She could see that they believed Jonas. Her eyes filled with tears of frustration and pain.

And then she heard it again. A baby began to squall loudly. The sound was coming from the laundry. She shrugged off Colt's hand and ran down the steps. Jonas reached for her, but she managed to sweep past him. Grace. It was her baby crying for her. She knew that cry. She'd heard it in the middle of the night when the sisters had come for her breast milk. Somehow Grace had known she was here.

"Lola, don't," Jonas called after her. "Sister Rebecca, help Lola. She's going to hurt herself."

She could hear running footsteps behind her, but she was almost to the laundry-room door. Sister Rebecca had set off an alarm. As Lola burst into the room, a half dozen women were already looking in her direction. Lola paid them no mind. She ran toward the woman holding the baby.

Inside this room with the washers and dryers going, though she could barely hear the baby crying, all Lola could think about was getting to the woman before they hid Grace away again. Reaching the woman, she heard the infant let out a fresh squall as if the mother had pinched the poor thing.

Lola grabbed for the baby, but the woman swung around so all she got was a handful of dress cloth from the woman's shoulder.

"Lola, stop." It was the sheriff's voice as he stepped between her and the woman with the child. "May I see your baby," he said to the woman.

Chapter Six

Colt watched the woman with the infant look at Jonas standing in the doorway. The leader nodded that she should let the sheriff look. Colt held his breath as the woman turned so they could see the baby she held. The infant had stopped crying and now looked at them with big blue eyes fringed with tear-jeweled lashes.

"Grace?" Lola whispered as she tried to see the baby.

"May I?" the sheriff asked, and held out his arms.

After getting Jonas's permission, the woman released the baby to Flint. He carefully pulled back the knitted blanket the infant was wrapped in. Colt found himself holding his breath.

The sheriff peeked under the gown the baby

wore. Colt knew he was looking for the small heart-shaped birthmark that Lola had told him about. He checked under the baby's diaper. His shoulders fell a little as he looked up at Lola and shook his head. "It's a little boy."

"No," Lola cried. "I heard my baby. This isn't the baby I heard crying. It can't be. Sister Rebecca pulled the alarm. She warned them to hide my baby." She looked from the sheriff to Colt and back again before bursting into tears.

Colt stepped to her and pulled her into his arms. She cried against his chest as he looked past her to the sheriff. He'd watched the whole thing play out, holding his breath. The baby the sheriff had taken from the woman was adorable and about the right age. Was it possible Lola was wrong about the sex of the infant she'd given birth to? Maybe the baby hadn't died.

But Lola had been so sure it was a little girl. She'd convinced him. And there was the tiny heart birthmark that Lola had seen on their daughter. But what if she was wrong and Jonas was telling the truth about all of it?

Now he felt sick. He thought of the small grave next to Lola's parents'. He felt such a sense of loss that it made him ache inside. He pulled Lola tighter to him, feeling her heart breaking along with his own.

As the sheriff spoke again with Jonas, Colt led Lola out of the laundry and down the path toward his pickup.

"I heard her," she said between sobs. "The first baby I heard. It was Grace. I know her cry. A mother knows her baby's cry. Sister Rebecca pulled the alarm to warn them so they could hide her again." She began to cry again as he led her to the truck and opened the passenger-side door for her. "Please, Colt, we can't leave without our baby."

He tried to think of what to say, but his throat had closed with all the emotions he was feeling, an incredible sense of loss and regret. It broke his heart to see Lola like this.

Lola met his gaze with a look that felt like an arrow to his chest before she climbed into the pickup. As he closed the passenger-side door, the sheriff walked over. "You all right?" Flint asked.

All Colt could do was nod. He wasn't sure he would ever be all right.

"I think we're done here," the sheriff said. "If you want to take it further…"

He shook his head. "Thanks for your help,"

he managed to get out before walking around to the driver's side of his pickup. As he slid behind the wheel, he saw that Lola had dried her tears and was now sitting ramrod straight in her seat with that same look of surrender that tore at him.

He started the engine, unable to look at her.

"You don't believe me. You believe…" She stopped and he looked over at her. She was staring straight ahead. He followed her gaze to where Jonas was standing on the porch of the main building. There was both sympathy and pity in the man's gaze. "He's lying." But Lola said it with little conviction as Colt started the pickup and headed off the compound.

LOLA CLOSED HER EYES and leaned back against the pickup as they headed down the mountain road. What had she expected? That Jonas would just hand over Grace? She'd been such a fool. Worse, she feared that they'd made things worse for Grace—not to mention the way Colt had looked at her. Leaving them alone with Jonas had been the wrong thing to do. She knew what that man was like. Of course the sheriff would believe anything the leader told him. But Colt?

"What did Jonas tell you?" She had to ask as she squeezed her eyes shut tighter, unable to look at him. "That I'm crazy?"

"He said your baby died. That it was a little boy. He showed me the grave."

She let out a muffled cry and opened her eyes. Staring straight ahead at the narrow dirt road that wound down the mountain, she said, "Is that what convinced you I was lying?"

"Why didn't you tell me you were on prescription medication?" Colt asked.

She let out a bark of a laugh. "Of course, my *medication*. What did he tell you it was for?"

"He hinted it was for schizophrenia and that after your breakdown—"

"Right—my breakdown. What else?"

He glanced over at her. "He said you were fired from your teaching job."

Tears blurred her eyes. She bit her lower lip and drew blood. "That at least is true. I resisted the advances of the school principal. When some materials in my classroom went missing, I was fired. Three days later, I heard that my parents had died. Perfect timing," she said sarcastically. "I'm not a thief. I wouldn't give in, so she did what she said she would, she fired me, claiming I stole the materials.

It was my word against hers—even though it wasn't the first time something like that had happened involving her. I had planned to fight it once I took care of getting my parents remains returned to the California cemetery. So what else did Jonas tell you about me?"

"That you're a troubled young woman."

"I am that," she agreed. "Given everything that has been done to me, I think that is understandable." Ahead she could see Brother Elmer waiting at the gate for them. Elmer was her father's age. When she'd first arrived at the compound, she'd asked him what had happened to her parents and Elmer had been too terrified to talk to her. She'd only had that one opportunity. Since then Elmer had kept his distance—just like the rest of them.

"Stop up here, please," Lola said, even though the gate was standing open.

Colt said nothing and did as she asked.

She put down the truck window as Colt pulled alongside the man. Elmer met her gaze for a moment before he dropped his head and stared at his feet. "Elmer, you know I'm not crazy. Help me, please," she pleaded. "You were my father's friend. Tell this man the truth about what really goes on back there in the compound."

Elmer continued to focus on the ground.

"Okay, just tell me this," she said, her voice cracking with emotion. "Is Grace all right? Are they taking good care of her?" She didn't expect an answer. She knew the cost of going against Jonas. Everyone did. If she was right and Jonas had had her parents killed…

Elmer raised his head slowly. As he did, he grabbed hold of the side of the truck, curling his fingers over the open window frame. His fingers brushed her arm. His gaze rose to meet hers. He gave one quick nod and removed his hands.

"You should move on now so I can close this gate, Sister Lola."

COLT BLINKED, TELLING HIMSELF he hadn't just seen that. His heart beat like a war drum. He swore under his breath. He'd seen the man's short, quick nod. He'd seen the compassion in Elmer's eyes.

Jonas Emanuel was a liar.

Colt wasn't sure who he was more angry with, Jonas or himself. He'd bought into the man's bull. He'd *believed* him. But the man had been damned convincing. The grave. The pills. The crying baby that wasn't Grace.

Shifting the pickup into gear, he felt as if he'd been punched in the gut numerous times. He kept seeing that tiny grave, kept imagining his son, their son, lying in a homemade coffin under it—just as he kept seeing Lola sobbing hysterically in his arms after hearing what she thought was her baby crying.

"Lola."

"Please, just leave me alone," she said as she closed her window and tucked herself into the corner of the pickup seat as he pulled away, the gate closing behind him. When he looked over at her a few miles down the road, he saw that anger and frustration had given way to emotional exhaustion. With the sun streaming in the window, she'd fallen asleep.

Colt was thankful for the time alone. He replayed everything Lola had said, along with what Jonas had told him. He hadn't known what to believe because the man was that persuasive. Jonas had convinced the sheriff—and Flint Cahill was a shrewd lawman.

But as he looked over at the woman sleeping in his pickup, he felt his heart ache in ways he'd never experienced before. He would slay dragons for this woman. He wanted to turn around and go back and…

He couldn't let his emotions get the best of him. He never had before. But this woman had drawn him from the moment he'd met her. He thought about the fear he'd seen in her eyes that first night. There'd been no confusion, though. If anything, they'd both wanted to escape from the world that night and lose themselves in each other. And they had. He remembered her naked in his arms and felt a pull stronger than gravity.

Would he have believed her if she'd told him on that first night what was going on? Probably not. Look how easily he'd let Jonas fool him. Colt was still furious with himself. He would never again question anything she told him.

Glancing in the rearview mirror, he wasn't surprised to see that they were being followed. Everything she'd told him had been true.

So where was the child he and Lola had conceived? He couldn't bear the thought of Grace being in Jonas's hands. But he also knew that they couldn't go back there until they had a plan.

As he slowed on the outskirts of Gilt Edge,

Lola stirred. She shot him a glance as she sat up.

"Before we go back to the ranch, I thought we'd get something to eat," he said, keeping his eye on the large dark SUV a couple of car lengths behind them.

"There is no reason to take me back to the ranch. You can just pull over anywhere and let me out."

"I'm not going to do that."

"I can understand why you don't want to help me, but I'm not leaving town until—"

"You get Grace back."

She stared at him. "Are you mocking me?"

"Not at all," he said, and looked over at her. "I'm sorry. I should have believed you. But I do now."

Tears welled in her eyes and spilled down her cheeks. "You believe me about Grace?"

"I do. I saw that armed guard who let us through the gate. I saw him nod when you asked him about Grace."

She wiped at her tears. "Is that what changed your mind?"

"That and a lot of other things, once I had time to think about it. That first night, you were scared and running from something, but you weren't confused. Nor do I think you were confused the next morning. You checked my wallet to see who I was. You considered taking the four hundred dollars in it, but decided not to. Those were not the actions of a troubled, mentally unstable woman. Also, we're being followed."

Lola glanced in her side mirror. "How long has that vehicle been back there?"

"Since we left the compound."

She seemed to consider that. "Why follow us? If they wanted to know where you lived..."

"I think they are more interested in you than me, but I guess we'll find out soon enough. That's the other thing that made me believe you once I was away from Jonas's hocus-pocus disappearing-baby act. I saw guards armed with concealed weapons around the perimeter of the compound. While there might not be any razor wire and a high fence, that place is secure as Fort Knox."

"So how are we going to find Grace and get her out of there?"

"I don't know. I haven't worked that out yet."

She looked at him as if afraid of this change in his attitude. "The sheriff believes Jonas."

"I don't blame Flint. Jonas is quite convincing. He certainly had me going."

Lola let out a bitter laugh. "How do you think he got so many people to follow him to Montana? To give him all their money, to convince them that to find peace, they needed to give up everything—especially their minds and free will."

"Why wasn't he able to brainwash you?" he asked as he glanced in the rearview mirror. Their tail was still back there.

"I don't know. The meditation, the chanting, the affirmations on the path to peace and happiness? I blocked them out, thinking about anything else. Also, I didn't buy into any of it. I was surprised my father did. It's one reason I didn't see them for so many years. My father wrote me and I spoke with my mother some on the phone, but there was no way I was going to visit them on the compound and they never left except to move to Montana with SLS."

"How was it your father was one of the founding members if it wasn't like him to buy into Jonas's propaganda?"

"My father would have done anything to make my mother happy. That's why he didn't leave after he quit believing in Jonas. He wouldn't have left her there alone. I'm sure he finally saw what my mother couldn't. That Jonas was a fraud. I feel terrible for those lost years."

"The man at the gate…"

"Elmer? He and my father were friends. It's possible that, like my father, he has doubts about SLS and Jonas. Also, not everyone is easily brainwashed into believing everything Jonas says. They might believe he has a right to my child because he says so. But that doesn't mean some aren't sympathetic to a mother losing her baby, our baby, to Jonas."

"I still don't understand how Jonas thinks he can get away with this."

"Because he has."

He glanced over at her, seeing that she was right. Jonas did rule that compound like it was his own country, and because his society was considered a church, he was protected.

"He has Grace," she said. "He knows I can't live without her. Except he's wrong if he thinks I'll let him keep my child, let alone that I would ever be his wife."

Colt glanced over at her. "So he knows we'll be back."

Chapter Seven

Lola looked out the side window as the road skirted Gilt Edge. Her heart beat so loudly that she thought for sure Colt would be able to hear it. Tears stung her eyes, but this time they were tears of relief.

Colt believed her.

The liberation made her weak. She'd seen his face earlier in the laundry when the baby had turned out not to be hers. She'd seen the heart-wrenching sympathy in his gaze, as well as the pain. He'd been so sure at the moment that she was everything Jonas had told him. A mentally unstable woman who couldn't accept the death of the baby she'd carried for nine months. *His* baby.

But Colt had seen the truth. He'd seen Elmer's slight nod, and when he looked at everything, he knew she was telling the truth.

She wiped at her tears, determined not to give in to the need to cry her heart out. They still didn't have Grace. Her stomach ached with a need to hold her baby. Jonas had Grace and that alone terrified her. Would he hurt the baby to get back at her?

No. He'd fooled the sheriff. He would feel safe and superior. He would simply wait, knowing, as Colt said, that they'd be back. Or at least she would. Jonas thought he'd fooled Colt, too.

She tried to assure herself that Jonas wouldn't hurt Grace just to spite her. The baby was his only hope of getting Lola back to the compound. She'd looked into Jonas's eyes as they'd left. He hadn't given up on her being his wife. He would need Grace if he had any hope of making that happen.

At least that must be his thinking, she told herself. It would be a cold day in hell before she would ever succumb to the man. And only then so she could get close enough to kill him.

"Do you think Jonas knows I'm Grace's father?" Colt asked, dragging her out of her dark thoughts. "He looked me right in the eye and told me that you swore you didn't know who the father was."

"I did. I was afraid he'd come after you. Or send some of his men to hurt you—if not kill you. He was quite upset to realize I was pregnant. I told him I didn't know your name. You were just someone who'd helped me."

"Helped himself to you. Isn't that what Jonas thought?"

She shrugged. "He was so angry with me. I'm not sure when he decided he wanted my baby. Our baby."

"Well, he can't have her."

"We will get her back, won't we?"

He reached over and took her hand.

"I mean, if you dig up the grave and prove that—"

"Lola, that would take time and be very iffy. First off, that is probably what Jonas is expecting us to do. Second, even if we had proof that your baby didn't die, I'm not sure we could get a judge to send up an army to search the place for Grace."

"Then what do we do?" She felt close to tears again.

"The problem is that it is hard for the authorities to get involved in these types of pseudo-religious groups, especially when, according to Jonas, you're a member—and so were your parents. It's your word against Jonas's. So I'm afraid we're on our own. But that's not a bad thing." He smiled at her. "I'll do everything in my power and then some to bring Grace home to you."

She smiled and squeezed his hand, knowing that she could depend on Colt.

COLT PULLED UP in front of the Stagecoach Saloon on the outskirts of Gilt Edge. The large dark SUV that had been following them drove on past. He tried to see the driver, but the windows were tinted too dark. The license plate was covered with mud, no accident either, he figured.

But it didn't matter. He knew exactly where it had come from.

"The sheriff's brother and sister own this place," Colt said as he parked and turned off the engine. "They serve some of the best food in the area. I thought we'd have something to eat and talk. It shouldn't be that busy this time of the day."

Lola's stomach growled in answer, making him smile. "I thought I would never eat after Grace was taken from me. But soon I realized that I needed my strength if I had any hope of getting her back. Not that I was given much food on the compound."

They got out, Lola slowing to admire the place. "I love this stone building."

"It was one of the original stagecoach stops along here. Lillie Cahill bought it with her brother Darby, to preserve it." He pushed open the door and Lola stepped in.

"Something smells wonderful," she whispered to Colt as they made their way to an out-of-the way table by the window. All this time eating nothing but the swill that had come out of the compound kitchen had left her ravenous.

There were a few regulars at the bar but other than that, the place was empty. A man who resembled the sheriff came over to take their orders. He had Flint's dark hair and gray eyes and was equally good-looking. "Major McCloud," the young man said, grinning at Colt.

"Just Colt, thank you."

"I heard you were back. Welcome home. Again, so sorry about your father."

"Thanks, Darby." All of the Cahills had been at the funeral. Colt's father would have liked that. He'd always respected their father,

Ely Cahill, even though a lot of people in this town considered him a nut. "This is my friend Lola."

Darby turned to Lola and said, "Nice to meet you."

"Congrats on the marriage and fatherhood. How's your family?" Colt asked, since that's what small-town people did. Everyone knew everyone else. He was sure Darby had heard about Julia and Wyatt since they'd all gone to school together.

"Fine. Lillie's married and now has a son, TC. She married Trask Beaumont. If you're sticking around for a while, you'll have to meet Mariah and my son, Daniel. Don't know if Flint mentioned it, but his wife, Maggie... Yep. Expecting."

Colt laughed. "Must be somethin' in the water. Which reminds me. Ely still kickin'?"

Darby laughed. "Hasn't changed a bit. Still spends most of his time up in the mountains when he's not hanging around the missile silo." He sighed. "So what can I get you?"

"What's cooking today? Something smells delicious."

"Our cook, Billie Dee, whipped up one of her down-home Texas recipes. Today it's shrimp gumbo. Gotta warn ya, she's determined to add some spice in our lives and convert us Montanans."

"I'll have that," Lola and Colt said in unison, making Darby chuckle.

"Two coming up. What can I get you to drink?"

Colt looked at Lola. "Two colas?" She nodded and Darby went off to place their order.

"What was that about… Ely?"

"The Cahill patriarch. Famous in these parts because back in 1967, he swore he was abducted by aliens next to the missile silo on their ranch." Colt explained how the government had asked for two-acre plots around the area for defense back in the 1950s. "You might have seen that metal fence out in one of my pastures? There might be a live missile in it. No one but the government knows for sure."

"The missile silos on your property would be scary enough, but aliens?"

He laughed and nodded. "What makes Ely's story interesting to me is that night in 1967 the Air Force detected a flying-saucer type aircraft in the area. Lots of people saw it, including my father."

"So it's possible Ely is telling he truth as he knows it," she said, wide-eyed.

He shrugged. "I guess we'll never know for certain, but Ely swears it's true."

Darby brought their colas, and they sat in companionable silence for a few minutes.

"It feels so strange to be in a place like this," Lola said. "It's so...normal. I haven't had normal in way too long."

"How long had you been held at the compound before I met you in Billings?"

"Almost a month. The first week or so I was trying to get my parents' remains released to a mortuary in Gilt Edge. Jonas had been kind enough to offer me a place to stay until I could make arrangements. I didn't realize that he was lying to me until I tried to leave and realized there were armed guards keeping me there. At least I wasn't locked up in a cabin that time. I had the run of the place, or I would never have gotten away in the back of the van when the sisters drove to Billings."

And Colt would never have met her. They would never have made love and conceived Grace, Colt thought. Funny how things worked out.

Darby put some background music on the

jukebox. The sun coming in the window gave the place a golden glow. Colt had been here a few times when he was home on leave. He was happy for Lillie and Darby for making a go of the place.

"How did you manage to get away this last time?" he asked.

"I'd been hiding my pills under my tongue until Sister Amelia left my cabin. I would spit them out and poke them into a hole I'd found in the cabin wall. The night I escaped, I pretended to be sick and managed to distract Sister Rebecca. When she wasn't looking, I hid the fork that was on my tray. She didn't notice that it was missing when she took my tray and left. I used the fork to pick the lock on the window and went out that way."

Darby returned a few moments later, accompanied by a large woman with a Southern accent carrying two steaming bowls of shrimp gumbo.

"Billie Dee, meet Colt McCloud," Darby said as he joined them. "Colt and I go way back. He's an Army helicopter pilot who's finally returned home—at least for a while, and this is his friend Lola."

"Pleased to meet you," the woman with the Texas accent said. "Hope you like my gumbo."

"I know we will," Colt said, and took a bite.

"Not too spicy for you?" the cook asked with a laugh.

"As long as it doesn't melt the spoon, it's not too spicy for me," Colt said, and looked to Lola.

She had tasted the gumbo and was smiling. "It's perfect."

Billie Dee looked pleased. "Enjoy."

Darby refilled their colas and gave them pieces of Billie Dee's Texas chocolate sheet cake to convey both "welcome home" and "glad to meet you."

Left alone again, Colt asked, "How are you doing?"

Lola realized that she felt better than she had in a long time. Just having food in her stomach made her feel stronger and more able to hold off the fear and frustration. She needed her baby.

But Colt believed her, and that made all the difference in the world. That felt like a huge hurdle given how convincing Jonas could be. Even more so, she was glad that she hadn't been wrong about Colt. They'd only been together that one night, but she hadn't forgotten his kindness, his tenderness, his protectiveness. Just having someone she could depend on… Her heart swelled as she looked over at him. "We're going to get Grace back, aren't we?"

JONAS STOOD AT the window of his cabin. He'd had his cabin built on the side of the mountain so he could look down on the compound. For a man who'd started with nothing, he'd done all right. He often wished his father was still alive to see it.

"Look, you sanctimonious old son of a bitch. You, who so lacked faith that I would accomplish anything in my life. You, who died so poor that your congregation had to scrape up money to have you buried behind the church you'd served all those years. You, who always managed to cut me down as if you couldn't stand it that I might do better than you. Well, I did!"

Thinking about his father made his pulse rise dangerously. He had to be careful not to get upset. Stress made his condition worse. So much worse that some of his followers had started to notice.

He stepped over to the small table where he kept his medication. He swallowed a pill and waited for it to work. He tried not to think about the father who had kicked him out at sixteen. But it wasn't his old man who was causing the problem this time. It was Lola.

"Lola." Just saying her name churned up a warring mix of emotions that had been raging inside him for some time. Over the years, a variety of willing women had come to his bed in the night. He'd turned none of them away, but nor had he wanted any of them to keep for himself. Until Lola.

Her mother had shown him a photograph of her daughter back when Maxine and her husband, Ted, had joined SLS. The Society was just getting on its feet in those days. The Daytons' money had gone a long way to start things rolling.

Jonas had especially liked Maxine, since he knew she was the one calling the shots. Ted would do anything for his wife. And had. All Jonas had to do was steer Maxine in whatever direction he wanted her to go and Ted would come along as a willing participant. If only they were all that easy to manage, he thought now with a sigh.

The photo of Lola had caught him off guard. There was a sweetness, a purity in that young face, but it was what he saw in her eyes. A fire. A passion banked in those mesmerizing violet eyes that had made him want to be the one to release it.

He'd done everything he could to get the Daytons to bring Lola to the California ranch. But the foolish girl had taken off right after high school to attend a college abroad. She'd wanted to become a teacher. Jonas had groaned when Maxine told him, and he'd conveyed his thoughts.

I think she could be anything she wants to be with my help. I really want to help her meet her potential. Lola is destined to do so much more than teach. She and I could lead the world to a better place. She might be the one person who could bring peace to the world.

Maxine had loved it, but Lola hadn't been having any of it. Right after college she'd headed for the Virgin Islands to teach sixth-grade geography at a private school down there. What a waste, he'd thought, not just for Lola but for himself. He had imagined what he could do with a woman like that warming his bed at night. They could run SLS together.

Lola would bring in the men. He'd bring in the women. They could build an empire and live like royalty.

He'd known that Ted wasn't happy after the move to Montana. Jonas had heard him trying to get Maxine to leave. That was the first time that Jonas had realized that Ted had held out on him. Ted hadn't bought into SLS either mentally or financially. He hadn't turned over all his money. He'd set some aside for Lola, and no small amount, either.

Ted's dissatisfaction and attempts to get Maxine to leave hadn't fitted into Jonas's plan. He suddenly realized there was only one way to get Lola to come to him. Maxine and Ted would have to die—and soon.

Getting Maxine to sign a paper of her intentions to persuade Lola to marry him had taken only one private session with her. Maxine had bought into SLS hook, line and sinker. If she wanted to save her daughter... He'd promised to give Lola the kind of life her mother had only dreamed of. Then he'd had Ted and Maxine disposed of and, just as he'd planned, Lola flew to Montana, bringing all that fire inside her.

But he'd underestimated her. She was nothing like her mother. He'd thought that his charm, his wit, his sincerity would work on the daughter the way it had on her mother. That was where he'd made his first mistake, he thought now as he watched dusk settle over the compound.

There'd been a series of other mistakes that had led to her getting pregnant by another man. That was a blow he still reeled from. But it hadn't changed his determination to have Lola, one way or another. Not even some Army pilot/rancher could stop him. No, he had the one thing that Lola wanted more than life.

She would be back. And this time, she wouldn't be leaving here again.

Chapter Eight

After shrimp gumbo at the Stagecoach Saloon, Colt took them to the grocery store. He and Lola grabbed a cart and began to fill it with food. He loved her enthusiasm. After being locked up and nearly starved for so long, she was like a kid in a candy store.

"Do you like this?" she would ask as she picked up one item after another.

"Get whatever sounds good to you."

She scampered around, quickly filling the cart with food she obviously hadn't had for a while as he grabbed the basics: milk, bread, eggs, butter, bacon and syrup.

"I suspect you can live on pancakes," she said, eyeing what he'd added to the cart.

He'd only grinned, realizing that he'd never enjoyed grocery shopping as much as he had with her today. They felt almost like an old married couple as they left the store. He found himself smiling at Lola as she tore into a bag of potato chips before they even reached the pickup. He unloaded their haul and had started to replace the cart in the rack when he heard someone call his name.

"Colt?"

He froze at the sound of Julia's voice. Somehow he'd managed not to cross paths with her since he'd been back in town, but only because he'd shopped either very early or very late. He'd picked a bad day to run out of groceries, he thought now with a grimace.

"Colt?"

Lola set her potato chip bag in the back of the pickup bed and walked over to join him. He could feel her looking from him to Julia, wondering why he wasn't responding. With a silent curse, he turned to face the woman he'd been ready to marry a year ago.

Julia looked exactly the same. Her dark hair was shorter, making her brown eyes seem even darker. She looked good, slim and perfect in a dress and heels. Julia always liked to dress up—even to go to the grocery store.

Gold glittered at her ears, her neck and, of course, on her ring finger, along with the sizable diamond resting there. The one he'd bought hadn't been nearly as large.

He swore under his breath. As many times as he'd imagined what it would be like running into her again, he'd never imaged this. Lola was watching the two of them as if enjoying a tennis match.

Colt had hoped that he wouldn't feel anything, given what Julia had done to him. But he'd believed in this woman, believed they would share the rest of their lives; otherwise, he would never have asked her to marry him. It had taken him almost three years to pop the question. He'd wanted to be sure. What a fool he'd been.

"I heard you were back," Julia said, and glanced from him to Lola beside him. "I was so sorry to hear about your father. I was at the funeral…"

He'd seen her and managed to avoid her.

"How are you?" she asked, sounding as if she cared.

As if sensing who this woman was and

what she'd meant to him, Lola reached over and took his hand, squeezing it gently.

"I'm good," he said, squeezing back. "And you?"

"Fine." She looked again at his companion, her gaze going to their clasped hands.

"I heard you've put the ranch up for sale." Julia hesitated. She brushed a lock of her hair back from her forehead, looking not quite as confident. "Does this mean you're going back into the military?" His joining the Army's flight program had been a bone of contention between them.

He shook his head, as if what he planned to do was any of her business.

"I was just wondering," she said, no doubt seeing him clenching his teeth. "I was hoping that if you were staying around Gilt Edge we could…" Again she hesitated. "Maybe we could have a cup of coffee sometime and just talk."

Just talk the way they had before she'd had an affair with Wyatt? Or talk the way they had when she hadn't shown up at the airport to give him a ride home?

"Our last conversation…" Julia looked again at Lola for a moment. "It went so badly.

I'd left you messages. I had no way of knowing you hadn't gotten them or the letter I sent."

"You were clear enough on the phone the last time we talked," he said, wishing she would just say whatever it was she needed to say so he didn't have to keep standing there. He could tell that she was waiting for him to introduce her to Lola, but his heart was beating too hard. Julia and Wyatt had hurt him badly. Her and one of his friends? Equal amounts of anger and regret had him shaking inside.

But he didn't want to get into an argument here in the grocery store parking lot in front of Lola. He didn't want Julia to know just how much she and Wyatt had hurt him. And he feared that if he started in on her, he wouldn't be able to stop until all of his grief and rage and hurt came pouring out.

"I'm glad you're home." Julia looked from him to Lola again and forced a weak smile. "It was good to see you. If you change your mind about that cup of coffee…" She stood for a moment, looking awkward and unsure, something new for Julia, he thought. And he realized that she needed him to tell her it was okay, what she'd done. That he forgave her.

That he wanted her and Wyatt to be happy. Julia was struggling with the guilt.

That alone should have made him feel better, he thought as she turned and left them standing there. Instead, he felt as if he'd been ambushed by a speeding freight train.

"I'm sorry," Lola said as she let go of his hand.

He couldn't speak so merely nodded as he took the cart to the rack and quickly returned to the pickup. Lola grabbed her potato chips out of the back and joined him in the cab. He'd expected her to be full of questions.

Instead, she buckled up, holding the bag of potato chips as if she'd lost her appetite, and quietly let him process what had just happened. He was thankful to her for that. And for taking his hand back there.

"Thanks," he said, after he got the truck going and drove out of the parking lot.

"It was the first time you've seen her since...since the breakup." It wasn't a question, but he answered it anyway.

"I've managed to avoid her. Just my luck..." He shook his head.

"I can see how painful it is."

"I'm more angry than hurt."

Lola looked out the side window. "Betrayal is always painful." She hugged herself.

He glanced over at her, thinking what a strong, determined woman she was. Not the kind who would give up when things got a little tough.

"Julia turned out not to be the woman I thought she was," he said. "I'm better off without her."

Lola said nothing, no doubt sensing that no matter what he said, he wasn't completely over his former fiancée or what she had put him through.

It made him angry that his heart hadn't let go of the hurt. The anger he didn't mind living with for a while.

WHAT WOULD LOLA do now? That was the question Jonas knew he should be asking himself as he stepped back inside his warm, elegantly furnished cabin.

She must think him a complete fool. Her great escape. He let out a bark of a laugh. Did she really think she could have gotten away unless he'd let her? Sure, he'd had his men chase her with instructions to make sure that she got away.

He'd known she would run straight to the father of her baby. As if he hadn't known she was lying about not knowing who she'd lain with. He scoffed at the idea. Sister Rebecca had seen her with a man near the hotel bar that night. Unfortunately, Lola and the man had disappeared on the elevator too quickly.

But Rebecca had managed to get the information. Major Colt McCloud. An Army helicopter pilot. Jonas would ask what she could see in a man like that, but he wasn't that stupid. The man was good-looking, part cowboy, part flight jockey. He had just inherited a large ranch.

Not that Jonas had been certain Colt McCloud was the man who'd knocked Lola up. No, he hadn't known that until today when the man had shown up with Lola and the sheriff.

Lola was too bound up from her conservative upbringing to go to bed with just anyone. So she'd seen something beyond Colt McCloud's good looks. Jonas swore under his breath as he moved to the fireplace to throw on another log. Just the thought of the cowboy pilot made his blood boil. How dare the man come up here making demands.

Jonas thought he might have convinced Colt

that Lola was unstable and not to be believed. She'd certainly played into his plan perfectly when she'd lost it in the laundry room. But he couldn't be sure about Colt. The man was probably smitten with Lola and would want to believe her.

At least the sheriff wouldn't be returning. He'd been sufficiently convinced. Law enforcement always backed off when it came to churches. Just like the government did. He smiled at the thought of how he'd been able to build The Society of Lasting Serenity without anyone looking over his shoulder.

Until now.

"You could return the baby," Sister Rebecca had dared to say to him before the dust had even settled earlier today. "You know she'll be back if you don't."

"Mind your place," he'd snapped. He'd seen how jealous the older woman was of Lola. He suspected she'd been mean to her, cutting her rations, possibly even being physically abusive to her. He hadn't stopped it, wanting Sister Rebecca's loyalty.

But now he wondered how much longer he might be able to count on Rebecca. Once Lola was back—and she would be back—Sister Rebecca might have to be taken down a notch or two. Then again, maybe it was time to re-tire her. Not that she would ever be allowed to leave. She knew too much.

Strange how a valuable asset could so quickly become a liability.

As soon as he had Lola… Yes, he would dispose of Sister Rebecca. It would be almost like a wedding gift for his new wife. Not that he would tell Lola what had really happened to the older woman. Let her believe he'd given Rebecca a golden parachute and sent her off to some island to bask in the sun for the rest of her days.

He stared into the flames as the log he'd added began to crackle and spark. If he was Colt McCloud, what would he do? Jonas smiled to himself, then picked up the phone. "We're going to need more guards tonight, especially around the cemetery."

AFTER RUNNING INTO JULIA, Colt had known it was just a matter of time before he and Wyatt crossed paths. He'd promised himself that when it happened, when he finally did see his traitorous, former good friend, he would keep his cool. He wasn't going to lose his temper.

If Wyatt wanted Julia, a woman who would betray her fiancé while he was fighting a war oceans away, then she was all his.

He'd visualized seeing both of them, but even in his imagination, he hadn't known what he would do. He'd told himself that he would tell them both off, make them feel even more guilty, if possible, hurt them the way they had hurt him.

But look what had happened when he'd seen Julia. He'd been boiling inside, his heart pounding, anger and hurt a potent mixture. And he'd said none of what he'd planned. Instead, he hadn't wanted them to know how much they'd hurt him. Or even how angry he still was.

After seeing Julia, it made him wonder when it could happen with Wyatt. How would Wyatt react? He just hoped Lola wouldn't have to witness it again. Colt thought that Wyatt must be dreading the day when they would come face-to-face again as much as he was. Colt hoped he'd given Wyatt a few sleepless nights worrying about it. Because, in a town the size of Gilt Edge, a meeting had to happen.

But Colt was sorry that it had to happen at this moment as he stopped to get gas on the way out of town. Lola had gone inside the convenience mart to use the ladies' room.

As he stood filling the pickup with gas, Wyatt drove up, pulling to a pump two away from him.

Colt froze, his heart in this throat, as he watched Wyatt get out of his pickup and step to the fuel pump. He thought about staying where he was, pretending he never saw him. But that was way too cowardly. Anyway, he wanted to get this over with.

He finished fueling his truck and walked down the line of gas pumps. Wyatt looked up and saw him and seemed to freeze. They'd grown up together, hung out with many of the same friends since grade school. It was only after college that Colt, needing to do something more with his life, had enlisted in the Army helicopter program.

Wyatt had tried to talk him out of it. "Why do you need to go so far away? You're going to get yourself killed and for what?"

Colt hadn't been able to explain it to him. So he'd left to fly and fight while Wyatt had stayed on his family ranch and stolen Julia.

He took a step toward the man he'd thought he'd known better than himself. As he did, he wondered what he would come out of his mouth or if he would be able to speak. His pulse thundered in his ears as he advanced on his former friend.

"Colt." Wyatt was a big, strong cowboy. He put up both hands in surrender but held his ground. "Colt, whatever you're thinking—"

Colt hit him hard enough to drive him back a couple of steps. Wyatt banged into the side of his pickup.

"I don't want to fight you," Wyatt said as one large hand went to his bleeding nose.

"That's good," Colt said. "Since you'd probably take me." He knew that might be true since Wyatt had a few inches on him and a good twenty pounds, but as angry as he was, he'd fight like hell.

His hands were balled into fists, but he didn't hit him again. Wyatt's bleeding nose looked broken. Colt was reminded of the time Wyatt had taken on the school bully, a kid twice his size back then. His former friend was tough and had never backed down from a fight in all the time Colt had known him.

He took a step back, hating that he was remembering the years of their friendship. His eyes burned with tears, but damned if he was going to cry. Looking at Wyatt, he realized that losing Julia had hurt; losing someone he'd considered a close friend, though, had ripped out his heart.

He turned on his heel and walked back to his pickup before he made a complete fool of himself. His knuckles hurt, but nothing like his heart as he listened to Wyatt get into his truck and drive away.

LOLA HAD SEEN everything from the front window of the convenience store when she'd come back from the restroom. The "fight" had ended quickly enough.

She didn't have to ask who the man had been.

Wyatt Enderlin. When she'd asked Colt about him, he'd said they'd been friends. "It's a small town. We make friends for life here." She could imagine how much Wyatt's betrayal hurt Colt.

She pushed open the door and walked out to Colt's truck, climbing in without a word. Out of the corner of her eye, Lola saw him rub his skinned and swollen knuckles before he climbed behind the wheel.

It wasn't until they were in the pickup headed toward the ranch that Colt said, "You saw?"

She hesitated, forcing him to look over at her. "I wanted you to hit him again."

He smiled sadly at that. "I hadn't planned to even hit him once."

"Do you feel better or worse?"

Chuckling, he said, "Better and worse."

"Well, you got that out of the way."

"Right, I got to see them both on the same day. Lucky me." He drove in silence for a few minutes. "Wyatt and I were like brothers at one point growing up. I'd always wanted a brother…" He shook his head.

"He was your friend."

"*Was* being the key word here. My other friends like Darby Cahill never would have done that."

"Which hurts worse?" she finally asked.

Colt shot her a glance before turning back to his driving. "Wyatt."

"Maybe one day—"

"I don't think so. Being in the military you learn which men you can trust in battle. Those are the men you want watching your back. Wyatt, as it turned out, isn't one of them."

"I'm sorry." She let the words hang in the air for a moment. "Do you believe in fate?"

They were almost at the turnoff to the ranch. Ahead she could see the for-sale sign. They hadn't talked about it. She doubted they would because she already knew from the first time they'd met how Colt felt about flying the big birds in the military.

"Fate?" he asked, glancing at her for a moment before he slowed for the turn.

"Maybe it was fate that has brought us all to this point in our lives."

FATE? LOLA COULDN'T be serious. If his fate was having his fiancée hook up with his good friend behind his back, then he'd say he was one unlucky bastard. He said as much to Lola.

"I was thinking more about the way we met."

Instantly he hated having rained on her parade like that.

"If Julia hadn't broken up with you and had met you at the airport like she was supposed to, then you wouldn't have been in that hotel that night and I wouldn't have…"

Would some other man have saved her? Or taken advantage of a young woman who was obviously inexperienced and desperate? The thought made him sick to his stomach, but he wouldn't have known because he would never have laid eyes on Lola Dayton.

Nor would he be worrying about how to get their baby away from a madman at an armed and dangerous cult compound at the top of a mountain, he thought as he parked in front of the house at the ranch and shut off the engine.

But as he looked over at Lola, the anger he'd been feeling ebbed away. "You're right," he said, softening his tone as he reached over and squeezed her hand. "It definitely was fate that brought us together." Damn fickle fate, he thought, realizing with growing concern how much Lola was getting to him.

He put Julia, Wyatt and the past out of his mind and concentrated on what to do next. He knew what he was going to have to do. It went against his military training. A man didn't go in alone with no backup. Nor did he take matters into his own hands. He went through proper channels.

But there was no way the sheriff was going to be able to get a warrant to have whatever was buried on the church grounds exhumed— even if Colt could talk Flint into doing it.

Jonas would fight it and drag out the process. Meanwhile, that madman had their baby. Baby Grace, the daughter he had yet to lay eyes on.

After helping put the groceries away, he went into the ranch office. The maps were in a file—right where his father had kept them. He found the one he needed and spread it out on the desk.

"We need proof that Jonas is lying," Lola said from the open doorway.

"Proof won't do us any good. We need to find Grace and get her out of there."

"But that grave. If you dig it up—"

Colt shuddered at the thought. "That's exactly what Jonas will expect me to do." He recalled a shortage of manpower on the compound. But a woman could be just as deadly with a gun, he reminded himself. "While they're busy guarding the cemetery, I'll find Grace."

"I'm going with you," she said, stepping into the small office.

He shook his head, hating how intimate it felt with her in here. "It's going to be hard enough for me to get onto the grounds—and away again—without being caught."

"Exactly. They will expect you and will have doubled the guards. You're going to need me."

He started to argue, but she cut him off. "I have lived there all this time. I know the weakest spots along the perimeter. I also know the guards. And, maybe more important, I know where to look for Grace."

Admittedly, she made a good argument. "Lola, if we are both caught, no one will know we're up there. If Jonas is as dangerous as you think he is, we'll end up in the cemetery."

"If one of us is caught, then the other can distract them while whoever has Grace gets away."

He hated that her argument made sense, more sense than him trying to find Grace on his own. "Can you draw a map of the place?"

She nodded.

"Good. We leave at midnight."

LOLA HADN'T DARED HOPE, but as she watched Colt studying the web of old logging roads around the mountain compound on the map, she let herself believe they could succeed. They would get in, find Grace and slip back out with her. Once she had Grace in her arms, no way would she let anyone rip her out again. Especially Jonas.

"I'll need paper and a pen," she said as she

leaned over the desk. Their gazes met for a moment, his gaze deepening. She felt goose bumps ripple over her skin. Heat rushed to her center. Then he quickly looked away and began searching for what she needed.

She drew a map of the compound buildings, marking those that were used for housing. "I know you got a tour, but I thought this would help. As you can see there are two women's dorms, one for the women with babies. There is only the one men's dorm on the opposite side the main building."

"What's this?" Colt asked as he moved to her side to point at a large cabin away from the others and at the top of her diagram.

"Jonas's. He likes to look down on his followers."

"And this one at the bottom right?" His fingers brushed hers.

A shiver ran the length of her spine. She felt her nipples harden to pebbles under her top. "That's the storage room, shop and health center." Her voice cracked with emotion.

"And this one bottom left?" There was no doubt. He'd purposely brushed against her as he pointed to the only other structure. The bare skin of his arm was warm. His touch sent more shivers rippling through her. Her nipples ached inside her bra.

"Laundry." She turned enough to meet his eyes. What she saw made her molten inside. His gaze was dark with desire as his fingers trailed up her arm to brush against the side of her breast.

WHAT THE HELL are you doing? As if he could stop himself. He looked into Lola's beautiful violet gaze and knew he was lost. He wanted her. Needed her. Thought he would die if he didn't have her right now. This had been building inside him all day, he realized. Maybe since the first time he'd met her.

"Colt?" she breathed, and shuddered as his fingers brushed over the hard tip of her nipple. She moaned softly, her head going back to expose her slim silken neck.

He bent to kiss her throat, nipping at the pale skin, and felt her shiver before trailing kisses down into the hollow between her breasts. "Yes, Lola?" he asked, his muffled voice as filled with emotion as hers had been.

When she didn't answer, he raised his head to look into her eyes. He held her gaze, seeing the answer in all that lovely blue.

Cupping her other breast, he backed her up against the office wall and dropped his mouth to hers. Her lips parted and he took the invitation to let his tongue explore her as his free hand found the waistband of her jeans and slipped inside.

She let out a gasp as he found the sweet cleft between her legs. "Colt." This time it was a plea. She was wet. He began to stroke her, drawing back to look into her eyes. Her head was back and her mouth open. Tiny sounds escaped her lips as he slowly stroked, until he could feel her quiver against his fingers and finally cry out.

Withdrawing his hand, he swung her up into his arms and strode to his bedroom. He didn't want to think about later tonight when they would go up the mountain. Nor did he want to think about the future or even why he was doing this right now.

All he knew was that he wanted her more than his next breath. The only thing on his mind was making love to this woman who had captivated him from the first time he'd laid eyes on her.

Chapter Nine

Just before midnight, Lola and Colt loaded into his pickup and headed toward the SLS encampment. Colt had programmed his phone with the latest GPS information and had mapped out their best route up the mountain.

They'd both dressed in dark clothing. Lola had borrowed one of his black T-shirts. Her blond hair was pulled up under one of his black caps.

Earlier, after making love several times, they'd showered together, then sat down again with the map. His plan was to approach this like a battle.

Lola had showed him on her diagram what she thought was the best way in—and out again. The layout of the compound was star shaped, with the large main building at its center. It was where everyone ate, met for church and meetings, and where Jonas had his office.

From it, the other buildings formed the points of a star. At the top was Jonas's cabin, on the left center were the women's two dorms and on the right, the men's dorm. At the bottom was the laundry to the left and the health center, shop and storage building to the right.

"Once we grab Grace, someone will sound the alarm. Everyone will get a weapon and go to the edge of the property."

"The SLS is sounding less and less like a church by the moment," Colt had said.

"If the intruder or escapee is caught, a second signal will sound announcing the all clear," she'd said.

Colt had studied her for a moment. He couldn't help thinking of her earlier, naked in his arms. He wondered if he could ever get enough of this woman. "You're sure about this?"

She'd smiled, nodding. She really did have an amazing smile. "Whichever one of us has Grace gets out if the alarm goes off. Whoever doesn't have her distracts the guards to give them a chance to escape."

"Who will have Grace?" he'd asked.

"I guess it will depend on who finds her first. Once we approach the housing part, someone is bound to see us."

Colt would have preferred a more comprehensive plan. "You must have some idea where they are keeping Grace."

"Normally, she would be in the second women's dorm where the other babies are kept," she'd said. "But Jonas will know that I haven't given up. He might have ordered that Grace be kept in the other women's dorm."

"Where were they keeping you before you escaped?"

She'd drawn in a tiny box. "That's the cabin. It serves as the jail."

"And you could hear Grace crying when they came to pump your breast milk?" She'd nodded. "You're thinking they had our baby in this dorm, the farthest one to the west and closest to the cabin where you were being kept. I'll take that one, then head east to the second women's dorm if I don't see you. They won't expect us to come in from different directions."

"We'll meet up there. Or if the alarm goes off, just try to meet back at the pickup"

Now, as the road climbed up the mountain,

he looked over at Lola. She appeared calm. Her expression was one of determination. She was going after her baby. *Their* baby. Her last thought was her own safety.

His heart ached at the thought of their love-making. He couldn't let anything happen to this woman. Grace needed her. He needed her, he thought and pushed the thought away. What he needed was to get himself, Lola and their baby out of that compound alive tonight. Later he'd think about what he needed, what he wanted, what the hell he was going to do once Lola and Grace were safe.

The night was thankfully dark. Low clouds hunkered just over the tops of the tall ebony pines. No stars, let alone the moon, shone through. Colt thought they couldn't have picked a better night.

Still, he was anxious. So much was riding on this and he felt they were going in blind. What he did know had him both worried and scared. If Jonas or any of his followers caught them…

He couldn't let himself go down that trail of thought. If they wanted to get Grace out of there, they had no choice but to sneak in like thieves, find her and take her. Isn't that what Jonas had done?

LOLA HAD BEEN lost in thought when Colt pulled the pickup over, cut the engine and doused the lights. She'd been thinking about the ocean and the time she'd almost drowned.

Her father had saved her, plucking her from the depths and carrying her to the beach. She remembered lying on the warm sand staring up at the sky and gasping for breath as her father wept in relief over her.

She had no idea why that particular memory had surfaced now. Anything to keep her mind off what was about to happen once they reached the compound. She'd learned to let her mind wander during Jonas's attempts to brainwash her. She would think of anything but what was happening—just like now.

With the headlights off, they were pitched into blackness. She listened to the tick, tick, tick of the cooling engine, her heart a hammer in her chest.

"You ready?" he asked, his voice low and soft.

She nodded and locked gazes with him. Colt looked as if there was something he wanted to say. She'd seen that same look earlier after they'd made love.

Earlier, she'd put a finger to his lips. She hadn't wanted him to say the words that he thought he needed to say. Colt was an honorable man, but she couldn't let him say things that he'd later regret. Nor had she been able to bear the thought of him pouring his soul out to her at that moment. Just as now.

There was too much riding on what they were about to do. Emotions were high and had been since she'd appeared at his door in the middle of the night. There was no need to say anything then or now, though she understood his need. She too wanted to open her heart to him because both of them knew how dangerous this mission was. Neither of them might get out of this alive.

Just as he started to speak, she opened her door and stepped into the darkness. She gulped the cold spring-night air and fought her fear for Colt and their daughter, a gut-wrenching fear that made her eyes burn with tears.

COLT SAT FOR a moment alone in the cab of the dark pickup. What had he been about to say?

He shook his head. Lola had cut him off—just as she had earlier.

He sighed, wondering at this woman.

Then he got out, and the two of them headed through the dark pines for the hike to the compound.

They moved as silently as they could once their eyes adjusted to the darkness under the towering pines. A breeze stirred the boughs high above them, making the pines sigh.

Colt led the way until they were almost to the SLS property. The whole time, he'd been acutely aware of Lola behind him.

Now he stopped and motioned her forward. They stood inches apart for a long moment, listening.

Lola had suggested entering the property on the opposite side of the cemetery and the farthest away from any main road up to the mountaintop.

The main road was gated, so Jonas wouldn't be expecting them to come that way. That was also the most visible, so they'd opted for this approach.

But now it was time to separate. Colt could feel the tension in the air, as well as the tension between them. Lola had made it clear that she didn't want any words of undying love. But, after everything they'd shared, he felt the need to say something, do something.

He drew her close, looked into her violet eyes and kissed her.

"What was that?" she demanded in a whisper. "It felt like a goodbye kiss."

He shook his head and leaned close to whisper, "A promise to see you soon." As he drew back, he saw her smile. "Good luck," he whispered, and turned and headed in the opposite direction, his heart in his throat. If things didn't go well, he didn't want his last memory to be of her standing in the darkness, looking up at him with those big blue eyes and him not doing a damned thing.

Now he thought of her slightly gap-toothed smile and held it close to his heart for luck. Ahead he saw the no-trespassing sign and knew a guard wasn't far away.

LOLA TOUCHED HER TONGUE to her lower lip as she made her way through the pines. Just the thought of Colt's kiss made her heart beat a little faster. If she'd been falling for him before that moment, well, she'd just fallen a little further. She warned herself that this wasn't any way to go into a relationship.

Her mother would have called it "going in the back door." Maxine would not have approved of Lola having a baby out of wedlock when she could have married Jonas and given Grace a father.

But Grace did have a father. A fine father. Lola just didn't see them becoming a family. She shook the thought from her head and tried to concentrate. Getting Grace back, that was all that mattered.

She hadn't gone far when she saw a faint light bobbing through the trees ahead of her.

Ducking down, she watched as Elmer made his way along the edge of the property. She waited until he was well past her before she rose and sneaked onto the compound. The only lights were the ones outside the buildings that illuminated parts of the grounds.

Lola edged along the pines until she reached the edge of the men's dorm. Only one light shone at the front. She moved cautiously along the back, keeping to the dark shadows next to the building and being careful not to step on anything that might make a sound.

She had no desire to wake anyone, though

she thought the men's dorm was probably fairly empty. All of the men would be on guard duty tonight and maybe even some of the women.

Elmer would be turning back soon on his guard circuit. If she hurried, she should be able to reach the closest women's dorm and slip inside the nursery before he started back this way.

Before the first time she'd escaped, she'd had the run of the place, including the one women's dorm, where she'd stayed with the sisters. She'd even helped with the babies a few times. Because of that, she knew where to find the main nursery.

"If I find her first, how will I know her?" Colt had asked.

She'd smiled and said, "You'll know her and she'll know you."

"No, seriously."

"There were two babies born in the past six months that I know of. The boy we saw in the laundry and Grace."

At the end of the men's dorm, Lola stopped to listen. She heard nothing on the breeze. The distance between her and the women's dorms was a good dozen yards—all of them in the glow of the men's dorm light.

She looked for any movement in the darkness beyond. Seeing none, she sprinted the distance and dropped back into the shadows. Her heart pounded as she waited to see if she'd been spotted by one of the guards. The only one she'd seen was Elmer, but she knew there were others stationed around the compound, more than usual, just as she'd told Colt.

As she caught her breath, she thought of Colt and wondered where he was. Saying a silent prayer for his safety, she crept along the edge of the building to the door to the main nursery and grasping the knob, turned it.

COLT RECOGNIZED THE guard as one he'd seen here yesterday. The man looked tired and bored as he moved along the edge of the property and fiddled with the handgun holstered at his hip.

The guard had only gone a few feet when he stepped into the shadows and suddenly drew his weapon like an Old West gunfighter. He took the stance for a moment, pointing the gun into the darkness ahead of him and then holstered his weapon again as he moved on to practice his fast draw a few yards later.

Colt had been startled for a moment when the guard had suddenly drawn his weapon. He'd been more than a little relieved to see that the man's gun was pointing only at some imaginary person in the dark.

He slipped behind the man, closing the distance from the dense pines to the edge of the closest women's dorm. Stopping to listen, he heard a sound that froze him in place.

A low growl followed by another. This part of the country had its share of bear from black bear to grizzly. But the low growling sound he'd just heard wasn't coming from the darkness, he realized. Instead, it floated out of the open window on the back side of the women's dorm. Someone was snoring loudly.

It gave him good cover as he moved cautiously along the dark side of the building. Only a dim light shone inside. Staying as far back as possible, he peered in. The large room was filled with bunk beds like a military barrack. He recognized the woman in the closest lower bunk. Sister Alexa, a woman Colt had met in passing the day Jonas gave him the tour.

She let out a snort and stirred. He saw her eyes flicker and he froze. She blinked for a moment before her eyes fluttered shut and her snoring resumed.

Colt ducked away from the window and made his way down to the end that Lola said could house a second nursery. The outside light high over the front door of the main building cast a circle of golden light.

He watched from the dark shadows at the edge of the light. He'd only seen two guards so far, one on the way in and another crossing the complex, before he'd made his way to the far end of the building where he would find the nursery.

From where he stood, he could see toward the cemetery where Lola's parents were buried. He wondered about the small mound of fresh dirt next to them. Was something buried under there?

Jonas seemed like a man who didn't take chances. At the very least, he would have buried a small wooden casket. Colt remembered seeing the shop on his tour of the complex. Followers made wooden crosses in the shop that they sold when they went into town to raise money for the poor, Lola had told him.

She said she doubted the poor ever saw a dime of it.

"I think it's Jonas's way of keeping them busy and making a little extra cash. The crosses are crude, but I think people feel sorry for the followers and give them money."

He thought now about the small casket he'd seen in one corner of the shop during his tour and swallowed hard. What if Jonas had filled the casket under that mound of dirt since their visit?

The thought made his stomach roil. He pressed his back against the side of the women's dorm and waited for the guard he'd seen earlier to cross again.

From inside the women's dorm, he heard a baby begin to cry. His heart lodged in his throat. Grace?

LOLA TURNED THE knob slowly. The door creaked open an inch, then another. A small night-light shone from one corner of the room, illuminating four small cribs. In one of the cribs, a baby whimpered.

She looked toward the doorway into the sleeping room with its bunk beds. She could hear someone snoring softly, heard the rustle of covers and then silence.

Her heart pounded as she slipped through the door and into the nursery. The first two cribs were empty. She moved to the third one. The baby in it was small. A newborn. Sister Caroline's baby, she realized. Caroline had been due when Lola had run away from the compound that night.

She stepped to the last crib, looked down at the sleeping baby and felt her heart begin to pound.

COLT STOOD AGAINST the wall in the darkness outside the nursery. Inside, he heard the sound of footfalls as someone awakened in the dorm and headed for the nursery.

A few moments later, he heard a woman talking soothingly. The baby quit crying. He could hear the woman humming a tune to the child, but he didn't recognize the song.

Then again, he knew no children's songs. He tried to imagine himself getting up in the middle of the night to calm his crying infant and couldn't. It was so far from what he'd been doing for the last eleven years.

What kind of father would he make when

he didn't even know a song he could sing a child? Or could even imagine himself doing something like that? In all his years he'd never held a baby. He'd be afraid he would drop it with his big clumsy hands.

He could see the woman's shadow as she'd come into the room and now watched her swaying with the infant in her arms, singing softly, willing the baby back to sleep. Was the baby Grace?

He waited, staying to the dark shadow of the building as, in the distance, he saw the guard come back from making his rounds. The man was headed for the men's dorm. Change of shift? He hadn't anticipated that and realized he should have.

Where he was standing, the man would have to pass right by him. Colt had no chance of going undetected. Nor could he move away from the building without being seen.

Inside the nursery, he saw the shadow of the woman move. The singing continued as she seemed to lay the infant back into its crib. The man was getting closer now. His head was down. He looked tired, bored, ready to call it a night.

Where was his replacement? For all Colt

knew, there could be another guard headed from the opposite direction.

He realized the music had stopped inside the nursery. Reaching over, he tried the door. The knob turned in his hand.

He had no choice. He could stay where he was and be seen by the guard, or he could chance slipping into the nursery and coming face-to-face with the woman tending the baby.

He slipped into the nursery to find it empty except for four cribs lined up against one wall. As the door closed behind him, he heard voices outside. Two men. And then silence.

Colt waited a few more seconds before he approached the cribs and saw that all but one of the cribs was empty.

He moved quietly to the crib being used and looked down at the sleeping baby. The infant lay on its back, eyes closed. He carefully reached in and pulled up the homemade shift the baby wore.

FOR A MOMENT, Lola couldn't move or breathe. Her heart swelled to bursting as she looked down at the precious sleeping baby. She would have recognized her baby anywhere, but still, with trembling fingers, she lifted the hem of the infant's gown.

There on Grace's chubby little left thigh was the tiny heart-shaped birthmark. A sob rose in her throat. She desperately wanted to lift her daughter from the crib. For so long she'd yearned to hold her baby in her arms.

She tried to get control of her emotions, knowing that once she picked up Grace, she would have to move fast. With luck, Grace wouldn't cry. But being startled out of sleep she might, and it would set off an alarm that would awaken the women in the dorm, if not the whole complex.

Lola wiped at the warm tears on her cheeks as she stared at her daughter. Grace was beautiful, from her tiny bow-shaped mouth to her chubby cheeks. As if sensing her standing over the crib, Grace's eyes fluttered and she kicked with both legs.

Lola grabbed two of the baby blankets stacked next to the cribs. Reaching down, she hurriedly lifted her daughter. Grace started, her eyes coming wide-open in alarm.

Quickly wrapping her infant in the blankets, Lola turned toward the door and felt a hand drop to her shoulder.

Chapter Ten

Lola had been in midstep when the hand dropped to her shoulder. The fingers tightened, forcing her to stop. She turned, terrified of who she would find standing behind her.

Sister Amelia put a finger to her lips before Lola could speak. Their gazes locked for what seemed an eternity. Neither looked away until Grace stirred in Lola's arms.

"Go," Amelia whispered, and pushed her toward the door. From back in the dorm came the sound of footfalls. "Go!"

Lola stumbled out the door, Grace wrapped in a blanket and clutched to her chest. Behind her, she heard Sister Amelia say something to the woman who'd awakened. Then the door closed behind her and she was standing out in the dark of the building.

Run! The thought rippled through her, igniting her fight-or-flight impulse. She had Grace. If she could get her off the compound…

From the dark, she heard a sound. A whisper of movement. A dark shadow emerged and she saw it was one of the guards. She recognized him by the arrogant way he moved. Brother Zack. She'd seen the way the former military man looked at her when he thought no one was watching. She'd heard that he'd been drummed out of the service but could only guess for what. He'd struck fear in her the nights when she knew he was the guard working outside the cabin where she was being held.

If Sister Rebecca hadn't been in charge of her "rehabilitation" and had sisters coming every hour or so to chant over her, Lola feared what Brother Zack might have done.

Now she watched him move through the darkness, her heart in her throat. Had he seen her? He appeared to be headed right for her. From inside the baby blankets, Grace whimpered.

COLT CHECKED THE BABY. No heart-shaped birthmark on either chubby leg. The moment he lifted the thin gown, the baby began to kick. Its eyes came open. Colt froze, afraid to breathe. The baby's gaze became more unfocused. Its eyes slowly closed.

He took a breath and let it out slowly. Grace wasn't here. He stepped toward the door. The floor creaked under his boot. He froze again, listening. With a glance over his shoulder, he stepped to the door, pushed it open a few inches and slipped outside.

The dark night felt like a shroud over the complex. Only circles of golden light from the outside lamps illuminated a few spots around the complex. He waited for his eyes to adjust, keeping himself tucked back against the shadow of the building. Nothing seemed to move but the pine boughs in the breeze.

Off in the distance, an owl hooted, then the night fell silent again. He had no idea how long he'd been inside the nursery or where the guards might be now.

On the way in, he'd thought they'd been changing shifts. That meant the new ones might be more alert, having just started. He thought of Lola. She'd gone to the other women's dorm. Had she found Grace?

His fear was that Jonas would want the baby closer to him, knowing Lola wouldn't give up. But wouldn't he want one of the sisters watching over her? Jonas didn't seem like a hands-on father figure. Colt wondered if he, himself, was. He could only hope that Lola had already found Grace.

He looked around, but saw no one. It appeared that most of the guards were out by the cemetery. Jonas had thought Lola would try to get evidence to take to the sheriff. He had thought no one believed her—not even Colt. Maybe especially Colt.

He spotted one of the guards moving slowly through the pines out on the perimeter. He wanted desperately to go look for Lola, but they'd agreed that the best plan would be for them to meet at the pickup. That way if one of them was caught, the other could go for help rather than walk into a trap that would snare them both.

As soon as the guard was out of sight, Colt crossed between the buildings and worked his way along the dark side of the second women's dorm.

He reached the end of the building and looked to the expanse of open land he would have to cross to reach the dark safety of the pines.

As he started to take a step, he heard a

sound behind him and spun around to come face-to-face with Lola. One glance at her expression told him that the bundle in her arms was Grace.

She took a step toward him, smiling, tears in her eyes, and suddenly the night came alive with the shrill scream of an alarm.

LOLA FELT GRACE start at the horrible sound. From inside the blankets, the baby began to cry. Lola tore the blankets from the crying baby and thrust Grace's wriggling small body at Colt. "Take her and go!" she cried. "Go! I'll distract them." She could see that he wanted to argue. "Please."

He grabbed the now-screaming baby and, turning toward the pines, ran.

Lola felt a fist close on her heart as she looked down at the empty blanket in her hand. She didn't have time for regrets. She'd gotten to see her daughter, hold her for a few priceless minutes, but now she had to move, and she knew the best way to make the alarm stop.

Grabbing up several large stones lying along the side of the building's foundation, she quickly wrapped them in the baby blankets, then hugged the bundle against her chest.

It wouldn't fool anyone who got too close, but it might work long enough to get her where she needed to go.

Turning, she hurried back toward the center of the compound. She desperately needed to distract the guards and give Colt a chance to escape with Grace.

SLS members poured out of the dorms in their nightwear. She half ran toward Jonas's cabin, screaming at the top of her lungs. Guards came running from all directions.

Zack saw her and charged her. He would have taken her down, but Jonas had come out of his cabin. Seeing what was happening, he shut off the alarm with his cell phone.

"Leave her alone, Brother Zack!" he yelled down. "Don't hurt the baby."

Zack stopped just inches from her. She could see his disappointment. He hadn't cared if he hurt the baby. He had been looking forward to getting his hands on her.

"Bring her to me," Jonas ordered.

Zack reached for her, but she jerked back her arm. One of the rocks shifted and she had to grip her bundle harder.

"Never mind, Brother Zack," Jonas called down. "Lola, I know you don't want to hurt the baby. Come up to my cabin. I promise I won't hurt you or the child."

As if she believed a word out of his mouth. But she walked slowly up the hill, holding the bundle of rocks protectively against her breast.

She listened to make sure that none of the guards had stumbled across Colt and Grace. But there'd been no more activity at the edge of the complex, no shouts, no gunshots. Jonas had sounded the all clear siren. His followers were slowly wandering back to either their beds or their guard duty.

Before she reached the steps to the cabin, Jonas told Zack to leave only a few guards on duty. The rest, he said, could go to bed for what was left of the night.

Clearly he thought that the danger was over and that Lola had acted alone.

She stopped at the bottom of the porch steps and looked up at Jonas. He had a self-satisfied look on his face. He thought he'd won. He thought he had her and he had Grace.

"How did you get here?" Jonas asked suddenly, looking past her.

"I stole his pickup."

"Colt McCloud's? I thought he was your hero?" he mocked.

"Some hero," she said. "But that doesn't surprise you, does it? You knew he'd believe you and not me."

Jonas almost looked sorry for her. "The man's a fool."

She hugged the bundle tighter.

"You should come in. It's cold out here," he said. "Is the baby all right?"

She knew he had to be wondering how Grace had been able to sleep through all of the racket. He had to be getting suspicious.

"She is so sweet," Lola said, glancing down for a moment to peel back of the edge of the blanket so only she could see what was inside. She smiled down at the rock. "She really is an angel." She wanted to give Colt as much time as possible to get away with Grace, but she knew she couldn't keep standing out here or Jonas was going to become suspicious.

"As I've said all along," he agreed as she mounted the steps. He reached for the baby, but she turned to the side, holding the bundle away from him.

"Please, let me hold her just a little longer." Tears filled her eyes at just the thought of the few minutes she'd had Grace in her arms and the thought that they might be all she was going to get.

Jonas relented. "Of course, hold her all you want. There is no reason you should be separated from your child. If you stay here, you will have her all the time. Imagine what your life could be like here with me."

"I have." She hoped she kept the sarcasm out of the voice as she moved to the middle of the room, giving herself a little elbow room.

"We could travel. Europe, the Caribbean, anywhere your heart desired. We could take Angel with us."

"Her name is Grace."

He ignored that as he started to close the door. He froze and cocked his head, taking in the bundle in her arms again. "It really is amazing she slept through all of that noise," he said again.

"She knows she's with her mother now. She knows she's safe."

Jonas looked out the still-open doorway as if suddenly not so sure about being alone with her. She saw Zack watching them.

Lola knew she had no choice. Zack was watching, expecting trouble, and Jonas was getting suspicious. She had no choice.

"Europe? I love Europe," she said, and saw Jonas relax a little. He waved Zack away and closed the door. She looked around, remembering the last time she'd been brought here. Jonas had told her that he would make her his wife—one way or another. He'd tried to kiss her and she'd kicked him hard enough in the shin to get away and, apparently, given him a permanent limp.

Behind her, she heard him lock the door and limp toward her.

Chapter Eleven

Colt reached the pickup. All the way, he'd hoped that he would find Lola waiting for him even though he knew there was little chance of that.

Still, he was disappointed when he got there to find he was alone. Grace had quit crying not long after they'd left the compound. He was grateful for that since he was sure it had helped him get away.

He opened the passenger-side door, the dome light coming on as he laid the bundle Lola had given him on the seat to get his first look at his daughter.

A pair of big blue eyes stared up at him. He lost his heart in that moment. He touched the perfect little cheek, soft as downy feathers. She did resemble Lola, but he thought he could see himself a little in her, too.

"Hi, Grace," he whispered, his voice breaking. Tears welled in his eyes. He swallowed the lump in this throat. He had the baby, but what now?

He turned off the dome light, realizing that if someone had followed him, they would be able to see him through the pines. He stared into the darkness, willing Lola to appear.

He had to assume that Jonas had her by now. He'd heard the alarm go off and then another signal, which he'd assumed must be the all clear. Why would Jonas sound it unless he'd thought there was nothing more to fear?

Which meant he had Lola. She'd sacrificed herself to save her daughter. Their daughter.

He looked toward the dark trees, silently pleading for that not to be the case. He needed her. Grace needed her.

They had Lola. He couldn't leave without her. But he couldn't go back for her with the baby for fear of getting caught.

Nor could he stay there much longer. If Jonas suspected she hadn't come alone…

"What are we going to do, Grace?" he asked as he wrapped her in his coat and watched her fall back to sleep.

WITH HER BACK to Jonas, Lola reached into the baby blanket with her free hand and slowly turned to face him.

"What really happened to my parents?"

He had been moving toward her but stopped. "They were getting old, confused toward the end. Your mother came down with the flu. It turned into pneumonia. Your father stayed by her side. She was getting better and then she just…died."

She nodded, knowing that it happened at her mother's age, and not believing a word of it. "And my father?"

"I think he died of grief. You had to know how he was with your mother. I don't think he could live without her."

That too happened with people her parents' age who had been married as long as they had. "You didn't have them killed?" She said it softly so he wouldn't think it was an accusation. It wasn't like she expected the truth.

"Lola." There was that disappointing sound in his voice again. He took a step toward her. "Why must you always think the worst of me? Your parents believed in me."

Well, at least her mother had—until he'd had her killed, Lola thought. She wondered if he'd done it himself and realized how silly that was. Of course, he hadn't. Her heart went out to her parents. She couldn't bear thinking about their last moments.

"I took care of your baby for you. I wouldn't hurt a hair on that sweet thing's head. Or on yours. Let me see her." He was close now, and she feared he would make a grab for the baby.

She loosened her hold on the baby blanket bundle a little and faced him, her hand closing tightly around the rock inside.

"Thank you for taking care of her," she said, letting her voice fill with emotion.

"I will take care of you, too—if you give me a chance." He was getting too near—within reaching distance.

She took a step toward him, closing the distance between them as she pretended to hold out the baby for him to take. She had to be close. She had to make it count. It was her only hope of getting out of here and being with Grace.

As Jonas opened his arms for the baby, she pulled out the rock and swung it at his head. He managed to deflect the blow partially with his hand—just enough to knock the rock from her hold.

But she'd swung hard enough that the rock kept going. It caught him in the temple. He stumbled back. She pulled out the second rock, dropping the baby blankets, as she swung again.

This time, he didn't get a chance to raise an arm. The rock connected with the side of his head. His blood splattered on the rock, on her hand. He stood for a moment, looking stunned, then he went down hard on the wood floor.

Lola didn't waste any time. For all she knew he could be out cold—or only momentarily stunned and soon sounding the alarm so the whole cult would be on her heels.

She ran just as she had before. Only this time, she wasn't leaving her baby behind.

COLT HAD NEVER had trouble making a decision under duress. He'd been forced to make quick ones flying a chopper in Afghanistan. But one thing he'd never done was leave a man behind.

He couldn't this time, either. He'd purposely not taken a weapon into the compound earlier. They'd needed to get Grace out clean, and that meant not killing anyone—even if it meant getting themselves killed.

Now he took the weapons he would need. He was changing the rules—just as he was sure Jonas was. Wrapped in his coat, he laid Grace down on the floorboard of the pickup. She would be plenty warm enough—as long as he came back in a reasonable amount of time.

Locking the pickup door, he turned back toward the woods and the SLS compound. He wasn't leaving without Lola. And this time, he was armed and ready to fight his way in and out of the place if he had to.

LOLA FELT A sense of déjà vu as she ran through the woods. Her pulse hammered in her ears, her breath coming out in gasps. And yet she listened for the sound of the alarm that would alert the SLS members to fill the woods. Jonas would not let her get away if he had to run her to ground himself.

If he was able.

She had no idea how badly he'd been hurt. Or if he was already hot on her heels.

She crashed through the darkness, shoving away pine boughs that whipped her face and body. Colt had said how important it was for them get in and out of the compound without causing any more harm than was necessary.

"We're the trespassers," he'd told her. "We're the ones who will get thrown in jail if we fail tonight. We need to get in there and out as clean as possible."

She thought about the blood on the rock and could see something staining her right hand as she ran. Jonas's blood. She hadn't gotten out clean. She might have killed him. A cry escaped her lips as her ankle turned under her and she fell hard.

She struggled to get up as she hurriedly wiped the blood on the dried pine needles she'd fallen into. But the moment she put pressure on her ankle, she knew she wasn't going far. She didn't think it was broken, but she also couldn't put any weight on it without excruciating pain.

Grace. Colt. She had to get to them. They would have left by now, but she couldn't stay here. She couldn't let Jonas or one of his sheep find her. If Jonas was still alive. The thought that she might have killed him made her shudder. It had been one thing to wish him dead, to think she could kill him to save her daughter, but to actually know that she might have killed the man…

She crawled over to a pine tree and used the trunk to get to her feet. As she started to take a step, she saw a figure suddenly appear out of the blackness of the trees.

Lola felt a sob rise in her throat. She'd never been so glad to see anyone in her life. Colt. He seemed just as overwhelmed with joy to see her. She'd thought he would have left—as per their plan. But he couldn't leave her.

Another sob rose as he ran to her, grabbed her and pulled her to him, holding her so tightly she could hardly breath. "Lola," he kept saying against her hair. "Lola."

She couldn't speak. Her throat had closed as she fought to hold back the tears of relief. As he let go, she stepped down on her bad ankle and let out a cry of pain.

"You're hurt. What is it?" he asked, his voice filled with concern.

"My ankle. I'm not sure I can walk."

He swung her up in his arms and carried her through the trees to the truck. She hadn't realized how close she was to where they'd parked it earlier.

She looked around, suddenly scared. "Grace? Where's Grace?"

He unlocked the passenger side of the pickup, opened the door and picked up a bundle wrapped in his coat. She heard a sound come from within the bundle as Colt helped her into the pickup and put Grace into her arms. The tears came now, a floodgate opening. No longer could she hold back.

Tears streaming down her face, she turned back the edge of Colt's coat, which was wrapped around the infant. "Grace," she said as Colt slid behind the wheel, started the truck and headed off the mountain.

Lola held her baby, watching her daughter's sweet face in the faint light as Grace fell back asleep. She thought she could stare into that face forever. For so long she'd feared she'd never see her again, never hold her. She wiped at her tears and looked over at Colt. He smiled and she could see the emotion in his face.

"Have you met your daughter?" she asked.

"I have," he said, his voice sounding rough. "We got acquainted while we were waiting for you, until I couldn't wait any longer and had to come looking for you."

"I'm so thankful you did."

"Let's go home," he said, his voice breaking.

Tears filled her eyes again as she looked from him to their daughter. She pulled Grace close as they left the mountain and headed toward the ranch. Home.

Chapter Twelve

Jonas came to, lying on his back in a pool of his own blood. His hand went to the side of his head and came away sticky. He stared for a few moments at his fingers, the tips bright red, before he tried to sit up.

His head swam, forcing him to remain where he was. He couldn't remember what had happened. Had he fallen? He'd been meaning to have one of the brothers fix that rug to keep the corner from turning up.

But from where he lay, he could see that the rug wasn't to blame. Not twelve inches from him sat a rock the size of a cantaloupe. A dark stain covered one side of it. Nearby was a baby blanket and another rock of similar size.

Memory flooded him along with a cold, deadly rage. The pain in his skull was nothing compared to the open wound of Lola's betrayal. His heart felt as if it had been ripped out of his chest.

He thought of those moments when she'd been holding what he thought was her infant in her arms. They'd been talking and she had made it sound as if she was weakening toward him. His heart had soared with hope that she was finally coming around. He had so much to offer her. Had she finally realized that she'd be a fool to turn him down?

He'd been so happy for those moments when he'd thought things were going to work out with her and even the baby. That other man's baby, but a baby Jonas was willing to raise as his own as long as Lola became his wife and submitted to him.

The shock when she'd pulled the rock from the baby blankets was still painfully fresh. It had taken him a moment, his arms outstretched as he'd reached to take her and the infant to his bosom. The shock, the disappointment, the disbelief had slowed his movements, letting the rock get past his defenses and stun him just long enough that she was able to pull out the second rock and hit him much harder.

He closed his eyes now. He was in so much

pain, but a thought wriggled its way through. His eyelids flew open. His mind felt perfectly clear, making him aware of the quiet. He recalled the alert alarm going off. When Lola had come to him with the baby... Yes, he recalled. He'd sounded the all clear signal.

Why hadn't there been another alert? He had to assume that Lola had gotten away. Gotten away with the baby. If she'd been caught, she would have been brought to him by now. And if Sister Rebecca had checked the crib and found the baby missing...

For a moment, he thought the alarm must have sounded while he'd been unconscious. But if that was true, then Brother Zack would have come to check on him and found him lying here, bleeding to death.

Two things suddenly became crystal clear. Even through the excruciating pain, he saw now that Lola couldn't have acted alone. She would have had help to get the baby off the compound. And her showing up at his door with what he thought was the baby was only a diversion.

He let out a bitter laugh. As persuasive as he'd been, it was just as he'd feared. He hadn't convinced Colt McCloud that the woman was unbalanced, that their baby boy had died, that he should leave Lola while he could.

Apparently, she'd been more convincing than he had been. He grimaced at the thought. Admittedly, he had to give her credit—her plan had worked. Or had it been Colt Mc-Cloud's plan? He closed his eyes, cursing the man to hell. Colt was a dead man.

But so was he, he realized, if he didn't get help. He was still bleeding and even more light-headed. He felt around for his cell phone to activate the alarm.

He had to turn his head to find it. The pain was so intense that he almost passed out. He closed his hand around the phone and, leaving bloody fingerprints, hit the button to activate the alarm.

His hand holding the phone dropped to his side as the air filled with the shrill cry of the alert. Any moment Brother Zack would come bursting through the door. He could always depend on Zack.

Unlike someone else, he thought, remembering his second realization. If he was right, Colt had taken the baby while Lola had pretended to be acting alone. The alarm had sounded and she had known that she couldn't get away. So she'd come up to Jonas's cabin with the rocks in the baby blankets.

But wouldn't someone have checked the baby's crib? And then wouldn't Sister Rebecca, who was responsible for the infant, have realized the baby was gone and summoned help? Pulled the alarm again?

As Brother Zack burst through the front door and rushed to him, Jonas felt the steel blade of betrayal cut even deeper. One of his flock had betrayed him.

Chapter Thirteen

Colt woke to find Lola and the baby sleeping peacefully next to him. He felt his heart do a bump in his chest. The sight filled him with a sense of joy. A sense that all was right in the world.

Last night on the way down the mountain he'd felt like they were a family. It was a strange feeling for a man who'd been so independent for so long. They'd been exhausted, Lola barely able to walk on her ankle. He'd gotten them both inside the house and safe as quickly as he could.

With Grace sleeping in the middle of his big bed, he'd taken a look at Lola's ankle. Not broken, but definitely sprained badly. He'd wrapped it, both of them simply looking at each other and smiling. They'd done it. They'd gotten Grace back.

He had questions, but they could wait. Or maybe he never had to know what had happened back at the compound. He told himself it was over. They had Grace. That was all the proof they needed against Jonas should he try to take either the baby or Lola back.

They'd gone to bed, Grace curled between them, and fallen asleep instantly.

At the sound of a vehicle, Colt wondered who would be coming by so early in the morning as he slipped out of bed and quickly dressed.

Someone was knocking at his front door by the time he reached it. He peered out, worried for a moment that he'd find Jonas Emanuel standing on his front step.

"Sheriff," Colt said as he opened the door.

"A moment of your time," Flint said.

Colt stepped back to let the sheriff enter the house. Flint glanced around, clearly looking for something.

He'd been wondering how Jonas was going to handle this. He'd thought Jonas wouldn't call in the sheriff about the events of last night. He still didn't think he would. But this was definitely not a social call.

"What can I help you with, Sheriff?"

Flint turned to give him his full attention. "Jonas reported a break-in at the SLS compound last night. I was wondering if you knew anything about that."

"Was anything taken?"

Flint smiled. "Apparently not. But Jonas was injured when he tried to apprehend one of the intruders."

That was news. Colt thought of Lola just down the hall still in bed with Grace. Last night when he was wrapping her ankle, he'd seen what looked like blood on her sleeve. But he hadn't want to ask what she'd had to go through to get away.

"He see who did it?" Colt asked.

"Apparently not," Flint said again.

Just then the sound of a baby crying could be heard down the hall toward the bedroom.

Flint froze.

"So nothing was taken," Colt said. "Jonas's injuries…"

"Aren't life-threatening at this point," Flint said as Lola limped down the hall from the bedroom, the baby in her arms.

Lola spotted the sheriff and stopped, her gaze flying to Colt. She looked worried until

Colt said, "You remember Lola. And this is our daughter, Grace."

Colt moved to her to take the baby. He stepped to the sheriff, turning back the blanket his daughter was nestled in.

Every time he saw her sweet face his heart swelled to overflowing. She was so precious. Having never changed a diaper in his life, he'd learned quickly last night.

Now he lifted the cotton gown she'd been wearing when Lola had taken her from the crib last night at SLS to expose the tiny heart-shaped birthmark.

"Our baby girl," Colt said. "We'll be going to the doctor later today to have her checked over—and a DNA test done, in case you were wondering."

Flint nodded solemnly, and Colt handed Grace back to Lola. As she limped into the kitchen with the baby, the sheriff said, "I'm not going to ask, but I hope you know what you're doing."

"That little girl belongs with her mother."

The sheriff met his gaze. "And her father?"

"I'm her father."

Flint sighed. "I was at the hospital this morning taking Jonas's statement. He isn't filing assault charges because he says he doesn't know who attacked him. I see Lola is limping."

Colt said nothing.

"You sure this is over?" the sheriff asked.

"It is as far as I'm concerned."

Flint nodded. "Not sure Jonas feels that way. Got the impression he's a man who is used to getting what he wants."

Colt couldn't have agreed more. "He can't have Lola and Grace, but I don't want any trouble."

The sheriff shook his head at that. "I'm afraid it won't be your choice."

He knew a warning when he heard one. Not that he had to be told that Jonas was dangerous. "He's brainwashed those people, taken their money and keeps them up on that mountain like prisoners."

Flint nodded. "A choice each of them made."

"Except for the children up there."

"You think I like any of what I saw on that mountain?" Flint swore. "But you also know there is nothing I can do about it. That's private property up there. Jonas has every right to keep trespassers off. Not to mention it is church property, holy ground under the law."

"I have no intention of going up there."

"I wish I thought it was that simple." The sheriff had taken off his Stetson when he'd come into the house, and now he settled his hat back on his head. Turning, he started for the door. "You know my number," he said over his shoulder. "I'll come as quickly as I can. But I fear even that could be too late."

"Thanks for stopping by, Sheriff."

At the door, Flint turned to look back at him. Lola had come out of the kitchen carrying the baby. She was smiling down at Grace, cooing softly.

Flint's expression softened and Colt remembered that Darby had mentioned the sheriff's wife was pregnant. "Have a good day," Flint said, and left.

JONAS LISTENED TO the doctor tell him how lucky he was. He had a monster headache and hated being flat on his back in the hospital when he had things that needed to be done— and quickly.

"You lost a lot of blood," the doctor was saying. "If your…friend hadn't gotten you here when he did…"

"Yes, it is fortunate that Brother Zack found

me when he did," Jonas said. He didn't need the doctor telling him how lucky he was. He was very aware. But a man made his own luck. He'd learned that when he'd left home to find his own way in life.

Not that he discounted what nature had given him—a handsome, honest-looking face, mesmerizing blue eyes and snake-oil-salesman charm. But he was the one who'd taken those gifts and used them to the best of his ability. Not that they always worked. Lola, a case in point. They'd worked enough, though, that he was a very rich man and, until recently, he would have said he had very loyal followers who saw to his every need. What more could a man ask for?

"You're going to have a headache for a while, but fortunately, you suffered only a minor concussion. A fall like that could have killed a man half your age. Like I said, lucky."

"Lucky," Jonas repeated. "Yes, Doctor, I was. So when can I be released?"

"Your laceration is healing quite nicely, but that bandage needs to be changed regularly so I'd prefer you stay in the hospital at least another day, maybe longer."

That was not what he wanted to hear. "One

of the sisters could change my bandage for me. Really, I would be much more comfortable in my own home. I have plenty of people to look after me."

The doctor wavered. Jonas knew that the hospital staff would be much more comfortable with him gone, as well. A half dozen of the brothers and some of the SLS sisters had been coming and going since his "accident." He'd seen the way the hospital staff looked at them, the men in their black pants and white shirts, the woman in their long shapeless white dresses.

"I'd prefer you stay another day at least. I'll give instructions to one of your...sisters for after that. We'll see how you're doing tomorrow."

"I'm feeling so much better. I promise that when you release me, I will rest and take care of myself." His head ached more than he had let the doctor know. He didn't want any medication that would make his brain fuzzy. He needed his wits about him now more than ever.

"Like I said, we'll see how you are tomorrow," the doctor said, eyeing him suspiciously. The man knew Jonas couldn't be feeling that good, not with his head almost bashed in. He also knew the doctor had to be questioning how he could have hurt himself like this in a fall.

Jonas just wished he would go away and leave him alone.

"I need to ask you about these pills you've been taking," the doctor said, clearly not leaving yet. "One of your church members told me they were for a bad heart, but that's not the medication you're taking."

"No, it's not for a heart ailment," Jonas had to admit. "I'd prefer my flock not worry about my health, Doctor."

"If you're suffering from memory loss at your age, then we need to run some tests and see—"

"I have early-onset Alzheimer's," Jonas interrupted.

The doctor blinked.

"It is in the beginning stages, thus the pills I'm taking. I can assure you that I'm being well taken care of."

The doctor seemed at a loss for words.

"I believe Brother Zack is waiting in the hall," Jonas said to the doctor. "Would you ask him to step in here? I need to talk to him."

Realizing he was excused, the doctor left. A few moments later, Zack stuck his head in the door.

Jonas motioned him in. "Close the door. Have you seen Sister Rebecca?"

"Not since last night."

"Who was on duty at the second nursery last night?" he asked.

Zack frowned. "Sister Alexa." His eyes widened as he realized what the leader was really asking. "Sister Rebecca was taking care of the...special baby."

The angel. That's what Jonas had told his flock. That he'd had a vision and Lola's baby was a chosen one.

"Sister Rebecca." Jonas nodded and closed his eyes for a moment. He'd known it, but had needed Zack to verify his suspicions. Rebecca had been with him since the beginning. If there was anyone he knew he could trust, could depend on, it was her. He slowly opened his eyes and stared up at the pale green ceiling.

Zack stood at the end of the bed, waiting. Rebecca and Zack had never gotten along. Jonas blamed it on simple jealousy. Both were in the top positions at SLS. He knew how much Zack was going to enjoy the task he was about to give him.

"Go back to the complex," Jonas told him. "I want Sister Rebecca—" if she was still there "—restrained. Use the cabin where Sister Lola stayed. Guard it yourself." He finally looked at Zack, who nodded, a malicious glint in his gaze even as he fought not to smile.

"I'll take care of it."

AFTER THE SHERIFF LEFT, Colt stepped to Lola and Grace and pulled them close. He knew the sheriff was worried and with good reason. Jonas was an egomaniac who enjoyed having power over other people. He ran his "church" like a fiefdom. He would be incensed to have lost Lola and the baby, but there was really nothing he could do. At least not legally. Once the DNA results came back, once they had proof that Grace was Colt's daughter…

He tried to put it out of his head. Jonas was in the hospital. He'd lied to the sheriff. It was over. Hopefully, the man would move on with some other obsession.

Colt cooked them breakfast while Lola fed Grace. He loved watching them together. It made his heart expand to near bursting.

Their day was quickly planned. First the DNA tests, then shopping for baby things. Never in his life had Colt thought about buying baby things, but now he realized he was excited. He wanted Grace to have whatever she needed.

At the doctor's office DNA samples were taken, then Colt took Lola and Grace to the small-box store on the edge of town. He was amazed at all the things a baby needed. Not just clothing and a car seat, but bottles and formula, baby food, diapers and wipes.

"How did babies survive before all of these things were on the market?" he joked, then insisted they get a changing table.

"It's too much," Lola said at one point.

"It's all good," he'd said, wanting only the best for his daughter. At the back of his mind, like a tiny devil perched on his shoulder, a voice was saying, "What are you doing? You are going back on assignment soon."

He shoved the thought aside, telling himself that he'd cross that bridge when he got there. He still had time. But time for what? There hadn't been any offers on the ranch. It was another thought that he pushed aside. Instead, he concentrated on Lola and Grace, enjoying being with them. Enjoying pretending at least for a while that they were a family.

He didn't even need the DNA test. That was all Lola. "We need it for Jonas should he ever try to take Grace again," she'd said. "Also, I don't want you to have doubts."

"I don't have any doubts."

She'd given him a dubious look. "I want it settled. Not that I will ever ask anything of you. And I will pay you back for all the baby things you bought. I called this morning and am having some money wired to me."

"That isn't necessary."

But she said nothing, a stubborn tilt to her chin. He hadn't argued.

Instead, he took them back to the Stagecoach Saloon where, the moment they walked in, he knew that Billie Dee was cooking up her famous Texas chili.

Lillie Cahill Beaumont just happened to be there visiting her brother, along with Darby and his wife, Mariah. They oohed and aahed over Grace and Lola did the same with their babies.

By the time they got home, Colt was ready for a nap, too. After Lola put Grace down, she came into the bedroom and curled up against him. He held her close, breathing in the scent of her. He'd never been more happy.

Chapter Fourteen

The next day, Jonas couldn't wait for the doctor to stop by so he could hopefully get out of the hospital. He knew that Zack was taking care of things on the complex, but he worried. He still couldn't believe that Rebecca would betray him. It shook the stable foundation that he'd built this life on. Never would he have suspected her of deceiving him.

When the doctor finally came by, he hadn't wanted to send Jonas home yet. It took a lot of lying to get the doctor to finally release him. It was late in the day before he finally got his discharge papers.

Elmer picked him up at the hospital and drove him to the compound. He liked Elmer, though he'd seen the man's faith in their work here fading. He and Lola's father had been friends. Jonas suspected Elmer only stayed because he had nowhere else to go. But that was all right. Jonas still thought that when the chips were down, he could depend on Elmer.

Once at the compound, Zack was waiting. Excusing Elmer, Jonas let Zack help him inside. He was weak and his head ached, but he was home. He had things that needed to be taken care of and had been going crazy in the hospital.

Three of the sisters entered his cabin, fussed over him until he couldn't take it any longer and sent them scurrying. The pain in his head was better. It was another pain that was riding him like a dark cloak on his shoulders.

As soon as he was settled, Jonas asked Zack to bring him Sister Rebecca. "She's still detained in the small cabin, right?"

"She is," Zack said.

"How is her…attitude?"

"Subdued."

Jonas almost laughed since it didn't seem like a word Zack would ever have used. "Subdued? Is she on anything?"

"No, but I've had the sisters chanting over her every few hours. I thought it was something you would have done yourself had you been here."

He was both touched and annoyed by Zack taking this step without his permission. But he needed Zack more than ever now so he let it go. "You did well. Thank you."

Zack beamed and Jonas saw something in the man's eyes that gave him pause. Zack wanted to lead SLS. The man actually thought he had what it took to do it. The realization was almost laughable.

"Bring Sister Rebecca to me," he said, and closed his eyes, his head pounding like a bass drum. He wondered if he shouldn't have put this off until he was feeling better.

Zack hurried out, leaving him peacefully alone with his thoughts. Lola had made a fool out of him by sleeping with Colt McCloud. To add to his embarrassment, she'd gotten pregnant. That child should have been his.

Instead, he'd put aside his hurt, his fury, his embarrassment and offered to raise the baby as his own. Still, she'd turned him down. How could she have humiliated him even more?

He let out a bark of a laugh. What had she done? She'd almost killed him—after giving him hope that she was weakening. The latter hurt the most. Offering hope was a poisonous pill that he'd swallowed in one big gulp. And now even his flock was turning against him.

Was he losing his mind faster than he'd thought? Could he trust his judgment?

He started at the knock on the door, forgetting for a moment that he'd been expecting it. "Come in."

The moment Rebecca walked through the door, he could see the guilt written all over her face. Brother Zack stood directly behind her. He started to step into the cabin, and Jonas could tell Zack thought he was going to get to watch this.

"That will be all, Zack."

The man looked surprised and then disappointed. But it was the flicker of anger he saw in Zack's eyes that caused concern.

Jonas watched his right-hand man slowly close the door, but he could tell he'd be standing outside hoping to hear whatever was going on. Was Zack now becoming a problem, too?

He saw Sister Rebecca quickly take him in. In her gaze shone concern and something even more disturbing—sympathy, if not pity. His head was still bandaged, dark stitches under the dressing, but his headaches were getting better. Stuck in the hospital, he'd had plenty of time to think over the past two days.

It was bad enough to be betrayed by Lola, even worse by Sister Rebecca, because he'd come to depend on her. She had to have known that Lola's baby had gone missing. It would have been the first thing she would have checked. Seeing the baby missing, she should have come to him.

He was anxious to talk to her, but as he looked at her standing there, he felt a loss of words for a moment. He kept telling himself that he was wrong. Sister Rebecca had been with him for years. She wouldn't betray him. Couldn't. He'd always thought she was half in love with him.

Which was probably why she hadn't come to him to let him know the baby wasn't in her crib. Even if she'd seen Lola with that bundle in her arms entering his cabin, she should have come to him. If she had, his head wouldn't be killing him right now. But he suspected Rebecca had wanted to be shed of Lola and the baby he was so determined to make his.

Since Zack had locked up Rebecca, she would know she was in trouble. He wondered what story she would tell him and how much of it he could believe?

COLT ALMOST CHANGED his mind. Things had been going so well that he didn't want or need the interruption. He enjoyed being with Lola and Grace. If he said so himself, he'd become proficient at diaper changes and getting chubby little limbs into onesies. He liked the middle-of-the-night feedings, holding Grace and watching her take her bottle. Her bright blue eyes watched him equally.

"I'm your daddy," he'd whispered last night, and felt a lump rise in his throat.

So when Julia had called and said it was important that they meet and talk, he hadn't been interested.

"If this is about you needing me to forgive you—"

"No. It's not that," she'd said quickly. "I doubt you can ever forgive me. I know how badly I hurt you."

Did she? The news had blindsided him. Hell, he'd been expecting her to pick him up at the airport—not break up with him to be with one of his friends. He still couldn't get his head around how that had gone down. No warning at all. He'd thought Wyatt hadn't even liked Julia. He knew that Darby didn't think she was right for him. Not that Darby had ever said anything. But Colt had been able to tell.

He could laugh now. He used to think that Darby just had his expectations set too high. But then Colt had met Mariah and realized that his friend had just been holding out for the real thing. Darby had done well.

"Julia, I can't see what meeting you for coffee could possibly—" It had been Lola who'd insisted he meet with Julia. She'd walked in while he was on the phone. As if gifted with ESP, she'd motioned to him that he should go.

"Fine," he'd said into the phone. "When and where?" He had just wanted to get it over with.

Now he drove past the coffee shop, telling himself that there was nothing Julia could say that would change anything. But she'd sounded...strange on the phone. He suspected something was up. Did he care, though?

He circled the block, saw a parking space and pulled his pickup in to it. For a moment he sat behind the wheel debating what he was about to do. And why had Lola been all for him seeing his ex? Was she worried that he wasn't over Julia? Or was she hoping to hook the two of them up again?

He'd heard her on the phone calling a car dealership to order a vehicle. "You don't have to do that. You can use my pickup whenever you want."

"I need my own car, but thank you," she'd said.

He thought of the discussion they'd had after he'd hung up from Julia.

"I knew that was Julia on the phone," Lola had said. "I wasn't eavesdropping. You talk to her in a certain way." She'd shrugged.

"A certain way?"

"I can't describe it, but you owe her nothing."

"Then why should I meet with her?"

"Because it won't be over until you tell her how you feel," Lola had said.

He had laughed. She made life seem so simple, and yet could her life have been any more complicated when he'd met her? "Okay, I'll meet with her with your blessing."

"You don't need my blessing."

He stepped to her and, taking her shoulders in his hands, pulled her close. "All I care about is you and Grace. You have to know that."

"So you'll talk to her. You'll be honest. You'll see if there is anything there that you might have missed. Or that you want back."

He'd wanted to argue the point, but she'd put a finger to his lips.

"You should go. She'll be waiting."

Let her wait, he thought now as he glanced at his watch. Let her think he wasn't coming—look how she'd treated him at the Billings airport.

Then, just wanting to be done with this, he climbed out and walked down to the coffee shop. It was midafternoon. Only a few tables were taken. Julia had chosen one at the back. Where no one would see the two of them together and report back to Wyatt?

As he pushed open the door, he saw her frowning down at her phone. Checking the time? Or reading a text from Wyatt?

She looked up as if sensing him and motioned him over. "I got you a coffee—just the way you like it."

Except he'd never liked his coffee that way. Julia had come out to the ranch when they'd first started dating with some caramel-mocha concoction. When he'd taken a sip, he'd had to force a smile and pretend he'd liked it. His mistake.

"It's good, huh. I thought you'd like it. You always have the same boring coffee. I thought we'd shake things up a bit," she'd said. And from then on, she'd decided that was the way he liked his coffee.

"Thanks," he said now, without sitting down, "But I never liked my coffee that way. I'll get my own." He moved to the counter and ordered a cup of black coffee before returning to the table.

She looked sullen, pouting like she used to when he'd displeased her—which was often enough that he knew this look too well.

"So what is it you want?" he asked as he sat down but didn't settle in. He didn't plan to stay long and was regretting coming here, no matter what Lola had said. He couldn't see how this could help anything.

Julia let out a nervous laugh. "This is not the way I saw this going."

"Oh?"

She seemed to regroup, drawing in a long breath, sitting up a little straighter. He was suddenly aware that she'd dressed up. He caught a hint of the perfume she used to wear when they were together because he'd commented one time that he liked it. He frowned as he realized she hadn't been wearing it the day they'd accidentally run into each other.

"What's going on, Julia?"

She looked away for a moment, biting down on the corner of her lower lip as if nervous. He used to think it was cute.

"I've made a terrible mistake. I didn't mean to blurt it out like that, but I can tell you're still angry and have no patience with me. Otherwise, you wouldn't have been so late, you would have drunk the coffee I ordered you and you wouldn't be looking at me as if you hated me."

He wasn't going to try to straighten her up on any of that. "Mistake?"

Julia looked at him as if she thought no one would be that daft. "Wyatt. I was just so lonely, and it looked as if you were never going to quit the military and come home…"

"How did you two get together? I always thought Wyatt didn't like you."

She mugged a face at him. "You don't need to be cruel."

"I'm serious. He never had a good word to

say about you. Or was he just trying to keep his feelings for you from me?"

"I have no idea. And I don't care. He probably didn't like me. Maybe that's why we aren't together anymore."

Colt realized he wasn't surprised. Julia hadn't gotten him to the altar. He remembered that had been the case with an earlier boyfriend, too. Looked like there was a pattern there, he thought but kept it to himself.

"That's too bad."

"I can tell that you're really broken up over it."

After the initial shock had worn off, he'd actually thought Julia and Wyatt wouldn't last. Julia was beautiful in a classic way, but definitely high maintenance. He could see that clearly after being around Lola. As for Wyatt, well, he'd never had a serious girlfriend. He'd always preferred playing the field, as he called it.

"I'm sincerely sorry it didn't work out. Is that all?"

"Colt, stop being so mean." She sounded close to tears. She glanced around to make sure no one had heard her. "I feel so bad about what I did to you."

"You shouldn't." He realized he meant it. For a while, he'd hoped she choked on the guilt daily. Now he didn't feel vindictive. He realized he no longer cared.

"I know how hurt you must be."

"I was hurt, Julia. That was one crushing blow you delivered, but I've moved on."

"With that woman you were with the other day? Are you in love with her?"

Now there was the question, wasn't it? "It's complicated."

"It doesn't have to be." She reached across the table and covered his hand.

He pulled his free. "Are you suggesting what I think you are?"

She looked at him as if to say, *No one can be this dense.* "I want you back. I'll do anything." She definitely sounded desperate.

Colt had played with this exact scheme in his mind on those long nights in the desert after she'd dumped him. It had been like a salve that made him feel better. Julia begging to come back to him. Him loving every minute of it before he turned her down flat.

Now it made him feel uncomfortable because he no longer wanted to hurt her. If anything, he felt indifferent and wondered what he'd ever seen in this woman. He couldn't help comparing her to Lola. Julia came up way short.

"Julia, you and I are never getting back together. Truthfully, I doubt we would have made it to the altar."

"How can you say that?" she demanded. "You asked me to marry you."

"I did. But I didn't realize then how wrong we were for each other. I overlooked things, thinking they would change once we were married. Now I know better. I'm sure it was the same for you. Otherwise, how could you have fallen so quickly in love with another man?"

She seemed at a loss for words.

"So I imagine we both would have realized we weren't right for each other before we made a huge mistake."

Julia stared at him as if looking at a stranger. "I don't believe this."

Had she expected him to take her back at the snap of her fingers? The flutter of her eyelashes? She really hadn't known him. Even if he'd never met Lola, he wouldn't have taken Julia back. She'd proved the kind of woman she was—not the kind a man could ever trust.

Colt got to his feet. "You should try to work things out with Wyatt. Now that I think about it, you two belong together."

Her eyes widened, then narrowed dangerously. "Do you realize what you're throwing away? And for what? That…that…woman I saw you with the other day?" She made a distasteful face.

"Easy, Julia," he said, lowering his voice. "You really don't want to say anything about the mother of my child."

"What?" she sputtered.

"Lola and I have a beautiful daughter together."

Openmouthed, she stared at him. "Lola? That's not possible. You can't have known her long enough to… Are you going to *marry* her?"

"I haven't asked her yet, but you know me. I like to take my time. Also, I'm a little gun-shy after my last engagement."

Julia pushed to her feet. He'd never seen her so angry. It made him want to laugh because he realized, with no small amount of relief, that had he married her, he would have seen her like this a lot.

The one thing he did know was that he

was completely over her. No hard feelings. No need for retribution. No need to ever see this woman again.

"This never happened," she said with a flip of her head. "You hear me? You're right. Wyatt and I are perfect together. We're going to get married and be happy."

He smiled. "So you and Wyatt aren't broken up." He let out a bark of a laugh. "Good to see that you haven't changed. Give Wyatt my regards."

Julia stormed out. Colt finished his coffee and threw away the cups Julia had left behind. He smiled as he headed for the door. He couldn't wait to get home to Lola and Grace.

Chapter Fifteen

Lola saw the change in Colt the moment he walked in the door. It was as if a weight had been lifted off his shoulders. He was smiling and seemed...happy.

"I guess I don't need to ask how it went." Her heart had been pounding ever since Julia's phone call. A woman knows. Julia wanted more than Colt's forgiveness. A woman like that would try to hold on to him, to keep him in the wings—if she didn't already want him back.

Colt met her gaze. "She wants me back."

It felt as if a fist had closed around her heart, but she fought not to let him see her pain. "That must seem like a dream come true."

He laughed. "I'll admit at one time it would have been. But no," he said with a shake of his head as he stepped to her. "It would never have happened even if I hadn't met you. But now that I have…" He leaned down to kiss her softly on the mouth. As he drew back, he saw that she was frowning.

"I don't want you giving up the woman you love because of me and Grace," she said quickly. "I told you. We can take care of ourselves."

"That wasn't what I meant." His blue-eyed gaze locked with hers and she felt a bolt of heat shoot to her core. "Julia is the last person on earth that I want."

She swallowed. "But you asked her to marry you."

"I did." He chuckled. "And I have no idea why I did. Honestly, I feel as if I dodged a bullet. But I don't want to talk about her. I want you," he said as he drew her close again. "Is Grace sleeping?"

While he'd been gone, Lola had practiced what she was going to say to him. But when she looked up into his blue gaze and saw the desire burning there, it ignited the blaze inside her.

She told herself that they could have a serious talk later. There was time. Colt was in such a good mood, she didn't want to bring him down. She cared too much about him. But that was the problem, wasn't it? She was falling in love with him. And that was why she and Grace had to leave before Colt did something stupid like ask her to stay.

LATER, AFTER MAKING LOVE and falling into a sated sleep, Colt heard Grace wake up from her nap and slipped out of bed to go see to her. "Hi, sweetheart," he said as he picked her up and carried her over to the changing table. As he changed her, he talked to her, telling her how pretty and sweet she was.

She was Lola in miniature, from her pert nose to her bow-shaped mouth to her violet eyes. And yet, he saw some of himself in the baby—and knew it might be only because he wanted it to be true. They hadn't gotten the DNA results, not that he was worried.

What bothered him was how much he wanted to see himself in Grace. How much he wanted to tell her about all the things he'd teach her as she grew up. What he wanted to do was talk about the future with Grace—and Lola.

Getting Lola's baby back was one thing,

but seeing himself in this equation? He would have said the last thing he needed was a family. He was selling the ranch and going back into the service. That had been his plan and he'd always had a plan.

Now he felt rudderless and aloft, not knowing if he was up or down. What would he do if not go back to flying choppers for the Army? Ranch?

He stared into Grace's adorable face, feeling his heart ache at the thought of being away from her. He picked her up, holding her as he felt his heart pounding next to hers. Fatherhood had always been so far off in the future. But now here it was looking back at him with so much trust... He thought of his own father, his parents' disastrous marriage, how disconnected he'd felt from both of them.

He knew nothing about being a father or a husband. A part of him felt guilty for asking Julia to marry him. True, he'd put her off for years. It had come down to break up or marry her. He'd thought it was what he'd wanted.

Now, though, he knew his heart hadn't been in it. What he'd told Julia earlier had been true. He doubted they would have made it to the altar. After he'd put that diamond—she'd picked it out herself—on her finger, all she'd talked about was the big wedding they would have, the big house, the big life.

He'd let her talk, not really taking her seriously. He should have, though.

While Lola… Well, she was different. Her heart was so filled with love for their child that she'd risked her life numerous times. He'd never met anyone like her. And Grace… She smiled and cooed up at him, her gaze meeting his, and he felt her steal another piece of his heart if she hadn't already taken it all.

"Does she need changing?" Lola asked from the doorway.

"All taken care of. She just smiled at me."

Lola laughed. "I saw that." She'd been watching from the doorway, he realized. He wondered how long she'd been there. She was wearing one of his shirts and, he'd bet, nothing under it. She couldn't have looked sexier.

His cell phone rang. Lola moved to him to take the baby.

After pulling out his phone, Colt felt a start when he saw that it was Margaret Barnes, his Realtor, calling. He'd forgotten about her, about listing the ranch. All that seemed like ages ago.

"Hello?" he said as he headed out of the nursery.

"Colt, I have some good news for you. I have a buyer for your ranch."

For a moment he couldn't speak. He looked back at Lola and Grace from the doorway. Lola was rocking the baby in her arms, smiling down at her, and Grace was cooing and smiling up at her mother—just as she had done moments before with her father.

"Colt, are you there?"

"Yes." He saw Lola look up as if she heard something in his voice.

"You said to find a buyer as quickly as I could. If you have some time today, stop by my office. I can get the paperwork all ready. The buyer is fine with your asking price and would like to take possession as soon as possible."

He felt as if the earth was crumbling under his feet. Yes, he'd told her to find a buyer and as quickly as possible. But that had been before. Before Lola had shown up at his door in the middle of the night. Before he'd known about Grace.

"What is it?" Lola asked, seeing his distress as she joined him in the living room. "Bad news?"

He stood holding his phone after disconnecting. "That was the Realtor."

Lola hadn't asked about the for-sale sign on the road into the ranch and he hadn't brought it up. But Lola knew what his plans had been months ago. The night they'd met he'd told her he was going to accept another Army assignment rather than resign his commission, like he'd been planning before that night, to marry Julia.

"Does she have a buyer for the ranch?" Lola asked, giving nothing away.

He wasn't sure what kind of reaction he'd been expecting. His gaze went to Grace in her arms. He felt his heart breaking. Lately, his only concern had been protecting Lola, getting Grace back and making sure that horrible Jonas didn't have either of them.

He hadn't thought about the future. Hadn't let himself. "I think we should talk about—" His phone rang again. He checked it, hoping it was the Realtor calling again. He'd tell her he needed more time.

It was the doctor calling. He glanced at

Lola and then picked up. "Doc?" he said into the phone.

"Your test results are back. You're welcome to come by and I would be happy to explain anything you didn't understand about DNA testing."

"Let's just cut to the chase, Doc."

Silence hung on the other end of the line for a long few moments. "The infant is a match for both Lola and you, Colt."

"Thanks, Doc." He looked to Lola, who didn't appear all that interested. Because she'd known all along.

"Are you all right?" she asked.

He nodded, but he wasn't. Grace had fallen back to sleep in her arms. Had there ever been a more beautiful, ethereal-looking child? No wonder Jonas had wanted her. Wanted her and Lola.

If he looked like a man in pain, he was. Lola and the baby had taken his already topsy-turvy life and given it a tailspin. All he'd wanted just days ago was to get out of this town, out of this state, out from under the ranch his father had left him and the responsibility that came with it.

Now, though, he no longer wanted to run.

He wanted to plant roots. He wanted to make them a family. "I think we should get married." The words were out and he wasn't sorry to hear them. But he should have done something romantic, not just blurted them out like that.

To his surprise, Lola smiled at him. "That's sweet, but…it's too early, isn't it?"

Too early? Like in the morning or—

"We hardly know each other."

"I'd say we know each other quite well," he said as he picked up the tail end of his shirt she was wearing.

She laughed and playfully slapped his hand away as she headed for the spare room that they'd made into a makeshift nursery. "You know what I mean."

He followed her and watched as she put Grace down in the crib. "We have a daughter."

"Yes, we do. But we can't get married just for Grace. You know that wouldn't work."

"But neither can I let the two of you walk out that door," he said.

"Colt, that door will soon be someone else's."

She had a point.

"I won't sell the ranch."

She gave him a pointed look. "I owe you

my life and Grace's. But I also owe you something else. Freedom. Grace and I can take care of ourselves now. Jonas is no longer a problem. He isn't going to bother us, not after the sheriff saw our daughter and knows that Jonas lied about keeping her from me. My parents set aside money for me should I ever need it and I saved the money I made teaching. Grace and I will be fine."

"But *I* won't be fine."

She looked at him, sympathy in her gaze.

"Lola, I need you. I need you and our daughter. I want us to be a family."

Tears welled in her eyes as she tried to pass him. "Colt."

He took her in his arms. "I know we haven't known each other long. But the night we met, we connected in a way that neither of us had before, right?" She nodded, though reluctantly it seemed. "And we've been through more than any couple can ever imagine, and yet we worked together and pulled it off against incredible odds. If any two people can make this work, it's you and me."

She smiled sweetly, but he could tell she wasn't convinced. "We're good together, I won't deny that. But, Colt, you don't want to ranch. You admitted that to me the first night we met. Now you're talking about keeping the ranch just to make a home for me and Grace? No, Colt. You would grow to resent us for tying you down. I see how your eyes light up when you talk about flying helicopters. That's what you love. That's where you need to be."

He wanted to argue, but he couldn't. She'd listened to him. She knew him better than even he knew himself. "Still—"

"No," she said as she moved down the hall-way to the room that they now shared. She began to pick up her clothing. "This is best and we both know it."

It didn't feel like the best thing to do. He'd come to look forward to seeing Lola's face each morning, hear her singing to the baby at night and spending his days with the two of them.

"Promise you won't leave just yet," he said, panicking at the sight of her getting her things ready.

She stopped and looked at him. "I'll stay until the ranch closes so you can spend as much time with Grace as possible. But then we have to go."

"It isn't just Grace I want to spend time

with," he said as he drew her close. He kissed her and told himself he'd figure out something. He had to. Because he couldn't bear the thought of either of them walking out of his life.

JONAS STUDIED THE woman before him, letting her wait. Sister Rebecca was what was known as a handsome woman. She stood almost six feet tall with straight brown hair cut chin-length. Close to his own age, she wasn't pretty, never had been. If anything, she was nondescript. You could pass her on the street and not see her.

That was one reason she'd worked out so well all these years. She didn't look dangerous. A person hardly noticed her. Until it was too late.

Studying her, Jonas admitted that he'd come to care very deeply for her. He had depended on her. Her betrayal cut him deeper even than Lola's. Fury gripped him like fingers around his throat.

Along with guilt, he saw something else in her face now. She knew that he knew what she'd done.

"Rebecca?"

She raised her gaze slowly. The moment she

met his eyes, her face seemed to crumble. She rushed to him to fall to her knees in front of his chair. "Forgive me, Father," she said, head bowed. "Please forgive me."

He didn't speak for a moment, couldn't. "For almost getting me killed or for letting Lola get away with the baby?"

She raised her head again. While pleas for forgiveness had streamed from her mouth, there was no sign of regret in her eyes.

"You stupid, foolish woman," he said with disgust, and pushed her away.

She fell back, landing hard. He watched as she slowly got to her feet. Her dark eyes were hard, her smile brittle. Defiance burned behind her gaze, a blaze that he saw had been burning for some time. Why hadn't he seen it? Because he'd been so consumed with Lola for so long.

"I have done whatever you've asked of me for years," she said, anger making her words sharp as knives hurled at him.

"As you should, as one of my followers," he snapped.

She let out a humorous laugh that sent a chill up his spine. "I wasn't just one of your followers."

He felt for his phone and realized he'd left

it over on the table, out of his reach. Zack had said he would be right outside the door. But would he be able to get in quickly enough if Rebecca attacked? Jonas knew he wasn't strong enough to fight her off. Rebecca probably knew it, too.

"Many times you were wrong, but still I did what you asked without question," she continued as she moved closer and closer until she was standing over him. "All these years, I've followed you, looked up to you, trusted that you were doing what was best for our community, best for me."

He swallowed, afraid he'd created a monster. If he was being honest, and now seemed like a good time for it, he'd let her think that one day the two of them would run SLS. He'd trusted her above all others, even Zack.

"You didn't sound the alarm when you found the crib empty," he said, trying to regain control and get the conversation back on safer ground.

She shook her head. "No, when I found Sister Amelia standing next to the empty crib, I told her to go back to bed and let me handle it. I thought about sounding the alarm, but then

I didn't. In truth? I was overjoyed to see the brat gone, along with her mother."

"That wasn't your decision to make."

She smiled at that. "You would destroy everything for that woman? You would take her bastard and raise it as your own? I thought of you as a god, but now I see that you are nothing but a man with a man's weaknesses."

The truth pierced his heart and he instantly recoiled. "You will not speak to me like this or there will be serious consequences."

A chuckle seemed to rise deep in her, coming out on a ragged breath. "Will you have the sisters chant more over me? You've already locked me up. Or…" Her gaze was hard as the stone Lola had used to try to bash his head in. "Will you have me killed? It wouldn't be the first time you've had a follower killed, would it?"

The threat was clear in her gaze, in her words. Rebecca knew too much. She could never leave this compound alive, and they both knew it.

He grabbed for his phone, but she reached it first. She held the phone away from him, stepping back, daring him to try to take it from her.

"This is ridiculous, Sister Rebecca. You would throw away everything we have worked so hard for out of simple jealousy?"

She raised a brow, but when she spoke her voice betrayed how close she was to tears again. This was breaking her heart as much as his own. "I know you. After all these years, I know you better than you know yourself. You'll go after her and that baby. You'll have her one way or another even if it means destroying everything."

He stared at her, hearing the truth in her words and realizing that he'd let her get too close. She *did* know him.

She looked down at the phone in her hand, then up at him. She pushed the alarm. The air on the mountaintop filled with the scream of the siren.

When Zack burst through the door, she threw Jonas his phone and, with one final look, turned and let Zack take her roughly by the arm and lead her back to her prison.

She wouldn't be locked up there long, Jonas thought. He owed her that at least, he thought as he sounded the all clear signal. But things weren't all right at all and he feared they never would be again.

Chapter Sixteen

Colt had been worried that the sheriff was right, that Jonas wasn't going to take what had happened lying down. Hearing that Jonas had been released from the hospital, he'd almost been expecting a visit from the SLS leader.

He'd been ready, a shotgun beside the door. But the day had passed without incident and so had the next and the next.

The days seemed to fly by since he'd signed the ranch papers and deposited a partial down payment from the buyer. He'd kept busy selling off the cattle and planning the auction for the farm equipment. He tried not to think about the liquidation of his father's legacy, telling himself his old man knew how much he hated ranching. It was his own fault for leaving Colt the ranch.

He was in the barn when he heard footfalls

behind him and turned to see Lola. "So the buyer doesn't want any of this?" she asked.

"No, I believe he plans to subdivide the property. It won't be a ranch at all anymore."

"And the house?"

"Demo it and put in a rental probably."

Lola said nothing, but when he saw her looking out the barn door toward the mountains, there was a wistfulness to her he couldn't ignore.

"I'm not leaving Montana. This will always be my home. I'm just not ranching. With what I got from the sale, I can do anything I want." But that was it. He didn't know what he wanted. His heart pulled him one way, then another.

"How long has your family owned this property?" she asked.

"My great-grandfather homesteaded it," he said. "I know it must sound disrespectful of me to sell it."

She shook her head. "It's yours to do with whatever you want, right?"

"Yes." He didn't bother to tell her that the three-month stipulation his father had put on it was over. "You were right. I'm not a rancher. I have no interest."

"But you're a cowboy."

He laughed. "That I will always be. I'm as at home on a horse as I am behind the controls of a helicopter. Ranching is a different animal altogether. Most ranchers now lease their land and let someone else worry about the critters, the drought, the price of hay. Few of them move cattle on horseback. They ride four-wheelers. Everyone seems to think ranching is romantic." He laughed at that. "It's the most boring job I've ever done in my life."

"That's why you're selling," she said with a smile. "It's the right thing."

He hadn't needed her permission, but he was thankful for it. As much as he denied it, there was guilt over selling something his father had fought for years to keep.

Nor had he contacted the Army about his next assignment, putting that off, as well. He still had plenty of leave, so there was time.

He'd also put off his Realtor about when the new owners could take possession. It sounded as if they hoped to raze the house as soon as he moved out.

He knew he couldn't keep avoiding giving

a firm date and time, but once that happened Lola and Grace would be gone.

"Where will you go?" he asked Lola.

"Probably back to California. At least for a while." The car she'd ordered had come, and she'd been able to get to her funds and make sure Jonas couldn't access them. She'd had to get a new driver's license since Jonas had taken her purse with hers inside, along with her passport and checkbook and credit cards.

Colt had heard her on the phone taking care of all that. No wonder he could feel the days slipping away until not only this ranch and the house he'd grown up in were gone, but also Lola and the baby. He worried that once he went back to the Army, this would feel like nothing more than a dream.

Yet, he knew that he would ache for Lola and Grace the rest of his life—if he let them get away. He'd always see their faces and yearn for them.

He'd never felt so confused in his life. What would he do if not go back to the Army? He was almost thirty-three. He couldn't retire even if he wanted to, which he didn't. He wanted to fly. But he couldn't ask Lola and Grace to wait for him for the next two to five years. He couldn't bear the thought of her worrying about him, or the worst happening and him never making it back.

His cell phone rang. Margaret again. "I'd better take this," he said to Lola. As she walked back toward the house, he picked up. "Margaret, I might have changed my mind."

Silence. "It's too late for that and you know it. Colt, what is this about?"

A woman and a child. The rest of my life. Regrets.

"If you're having second thoughts about selling the ranch—"

"I'm not. I just need a little more time to get off the property."

More silence. "I'll see what I can do but, Colt, they are getting very impatient. I need to tell these buyers something concrete. I can't keep putting them off or they are going to change their minds or fine you, which they can under the contract you signed." She sounded angry. He couldn't blame her.

As he looked out at the land, he had a thought. "I'll be in first thing in the morning."

"What does that mean?" she asked after a moment.

"I have an idea."

She groaned. "Could you be a touch more specific?"

"I'm selling the ranch, but there's something I need."

"Okay," she said slowly. "Why don't we sit down with them in the morning, if you're sure you won't change your mind."

He pocketed his phone and watched Lola as she slipped in the back door of the house. Taking off his Stetson, he wiped the sweat from his brow with his sleeve. "Do something," he said to himself. "Do something before it's too late."

"SHE'S STAYING ON the ranch with Colt Mc-Cloud," Zack told Jonas later that afternoon.

"Is the baby with them?"

"I've had the place watched as you ordered. They took the baby into town the next morning, bought baby clothes and supplies, and returned to the ranch."

So they were settling in. They thought it was over. "What kind of security?"

"No security system on the house. But I would imagine he has guns and knows how to use them since he's a major in the Army."

"I'm sure he does." That's why they would strike when the cowboy least expected it. He looked past Zack toward the main building below him on the hill. "You led church this morning?"

He nodded.

"What is the mood?"

Zack seemed to consider that. "Quite a few of them are upset over Sister Rebecca."

He'd suspected as much. "I'll lead the service tonight." Zack didn't appear to think that was going to make a difference. Jonas thought about the things that Rebecca had said and ground his teeth. He still had a headache, and while his wound was healing, it was a constant reminder of what Lola had done to him. Worse, she'd bewitched him, put a spell on him as if sent by the devil to bring him down.

Did he really want her back, or did he just want to retaliate? Did it matter in the long run? His memory was getting worse. The pills didn't seem to be working. He couldn't be sure how long he had until he was a blubbering old fool locked up in some rest home.

He shook his head. He wasn't going out that way. "I don't want Lola or the baby injured."

"What about McCloud?"

"Kill him and dispose of his body. I know the perfect place. If possible, leave no evidence that we were there."

COLT LEFT THE barn headed for the house, suddenly excited that his idea just might be the perfect plan. "Lola?" he cried as he burst through the back door.

"Colt?" She was standing in the kitchen wearing an apron that had belonged to his mother. He hadn't seen it in years. She must have found it in a drawer he and his father had obviously never bothered to look in.

"What?" she asked, seeing the way he was looking at her.

"You look so cute in that apron, that's all." He stepped to her. "I'm selling the ranch."

"I know."

"You were right. I'd make a terrible rancher, always did. This was my father's dream, not mine. I'm a helicopter pilot."

She nodded. "I thought we already knew this. So you're going to take the commission the Army is offering you."

"No."

She tilted her head. "No?"

"No," he said, smiling. "For years, my friend

Tommy and I have talked about starting our own helicopter service here in the state. We're good at what we do. With the money from the ranch, I can invest in the birds we'll need."

"That sounds right up your alley. But are you sure?"

He nodded. "Come here." He put his arm around her waist and ushered her over to the window. "Look out there. See that."

"Yes? That mountainside?"

"Imagine a house in that grove of aspens and pines. The view from there is incredible. Now imagine an office down by the road and a helipad. The office would be just a hop, skip and a jump from the house. We'd have everything we need for Grace and any other children we have."

LOLA SMILED AT HIM, caught up in his enthusiasm. "Isn't that land part of the ranch?"

He grinned. "I'm going to buy it back."

"Aren't you being a little impulsive?"

"Not at all. I've been thinking about this for years." He seemed to see what she meant and turned her to face him. "And I've been thinking about being with you since that first night. With you and Grace here… Lola, I've fallen for you and Grace…" He shook his head. "It was love at first sight even before I knew for certain that Grace was mine. I want you to stay. I want us to be a family."

"Colt, do you know what you're saying?" But it was what he wasn't saying that had her stomach in knots. She knew he wanted her and Grace, but she wouldn't let herself go into a loveless marriage just to give her daughter a home.

She said as much to him.

He stared at her. "Damn it, Lola, I love you."

She blinked in surprise. All their lovemaking, their quiet times together, those moments with Grace. She'd waited to hear those words. Well, maybe not the "damn it, Lola" part. But definitely the "I love you" part. Her heart had assured her that he loved her and Grace. And yet, she wouldn't let herself believe it was true until he finally told her.

"I love you," he repeated as if they were the most honest words he'd ever spoken. "I've only said those words twice to a woman. With Julia, it was over two years before I said them. I don't think it was a coincidence that I held off. With you… I've been wanting to say them for days now."

"Oh, Colt, I've been waiting to hear them. I love you, too."

He reached into his pocket and pulled out a small velvet box.

Lola gave a small gasp.

"This ring was handed down from my great-great-grandmother to my great-grandmother to my grandmother. When my grandmother gave it to me, she made me promise only to give it to a woman who was my equal." He opened the box.

She looked down at a beautiful thick gold band circled in diamonds. "Oh, Colt." Her gaze went to his. "I don't understand. Julia—"

"I didn't give it to her."

"Why?"

He shrugged. "I don't know. It didn't seem… right for her. She picked out one she liked uptown."

Her heart went out to him. Julia had hurt him badly in so many ways, only proving how wrong she was for him almost from the start.

"Now I realize that I was saving this ring so I could live up to the promise I made my grandmother," he said. "I want you to wear it."

He dropped to one knee. "Will you marry me, Lola Dayton, and be my wife and the mother to my children?"

She smiled through the burn of tears. "Yes."

He slipped the ring on her finger. It fit perfectly. "Now what is the chance of that?" he said to her, only making her cry and laugh at the same time.

Swinging her up into his arms, he spun her around and set her down gently. "For the first time in so long, I am excited about the future."

She could see that he'd been dragged down by the ranch, Julia and the past, as well as his need to do what he did so well—fly.

Colt kissed her softly on the mouth. She felt heat rush through her and, cupping his face in her hands, kissed him with the passion the man evoked in her.

He swung her up in his arms again, only this time he didn't put her down until they reached the bedroom.

THAT EVENING, JONAS held church in the main building. He'd gathered them all together to give them the news. He could feel the tension in the air. There'd been a time when he'd stood up here and felt as if he really was a god sent to this earth to lead desperate people looking for at least peace, if not salvation.

As he looked over his flock, though, all he felt was sad. His father used to say that all good things end. In this case, the preacher was right.

"Brothers and sisters. I have some sad news. As you know, Sister Rebecca has chosen to leave us. It is with a heavy heart that I had to let her go." He wondered how many of them knew the truth. Too many of them probably. He was glad he'd had Zack bury her far away from the compound.

"But that isn't the only news. I have decided that it is time to leave Montana." His words were followed by a murmur of concern that spread through his congregation. "As many of you know, I'm in poor health. My heart… I'm going to have to step down as your leader."

The murmurs rose. One woman called out, "What's to become of us?"

He'd bilked them out of all their money. A lot of them were old enough now that they would have a hard time getting a job. He didn't need this crowd turning on him as Sister Rebecca had.

"Brother Zack will be taking those who

want to go to property I've purchased in Arizona. It's farmable land, so you can maintain a life there. Each of you will be given a check to help with your expenses."

The murmur in the main building grew louder. "If you have any questions, please give those to Brother Zack. I trust him to make sure that each and every one of you will be taken care of." That quieted them down, either because they were assured or because they knew how Zack had taken care of other parishioners who'd became troublesome.

"It is with a heavy heart that I must step down, but I know that you all will be fine. You will leave tomorrow. Go with Godspeed." He turned and walked away, anxious to get back to his cabin and pack. The sale of his property would be enough to pay off his followers—not that he would be around to hear any complaints after tonight.

He rang for Zack. Since he'd told Zack of his plan, the man had been more than excited. Jonas had recognized that frenzied look in Zack's eyes. He'd seen it in his own. Zack would be Father Zack. God help his followers.

"I need you to pick about six brothers and a few sisters for a special mission," he told

Zack. It would be one of their last missions under him.

Zack nodded, clearly understanding that he needed to pick those who would still kill for their leader.

"Make sure one of them is Brother Elmer."

"Are you sure? I mean—"

"Already questioning my authority?" he asked with a chuckle.

"No, of course not."

"Good. I have my reasons."

"I'll get right on it," Zack said, and left him alone.

Jonas looked around the cabin. He'd had such hopes when he'd moved his flock to Montana. He couldn't get maudlin now. He had to think about his future. He stepped to the safe he had hidden in the wall, opened it and took out the large case he kept there full of cash and his passport. Next to it was Lola's purse.

He took that out, as well, and thumbed through it even though he knew exactly what was in it since he'd often looked through it. He liked touching her things. He found her passport. Good, it was up-to-date. He'd deal with getting the baby out of the country when it came time.

After putting Lola's passport beside his own into his case, he closed the safe. There was nothing keeping him here after tonight. He would have everything he'd ever dreamed of, including a small fortune waiting in foreign banks across the world.

He thought of his father, wishing he could see him now. "Go ahead, say it. You were right about me, you arrogant old sanctimonious fool. I was your worst nightmare and so much more. But you haven't seen anything yet."

Chapter Seventeen

Colt woke to the sound of both outside doors bursting open. The sudden noise woke the baby. Grace began to cry in the room down the hall. Lola stirred next to him and Colt, realizing what was happening, grabbed for his gun in the nightstand next to him.

Moments before he had lain in bed, with Lola beside him.

They were on him before he could draw the gun. They swept into the room, both men and women. Colt fought off the first couple of men, but a blow to the back of his head sent him to the floor and then they were on him, binding his hands behind him, gagging him, trussing his ankles and dragging him out of the house.

He tried to see Lola, but there was a group of women around her, helping her dress. In the baby's room, he heard Grace quiet and knew they had her, as well.

The strike had been so swift, so organized, that Colt realized he'd underestimated Zack—the only ex-military man in SLS. Clearly he had more experience at these kinds of maneuvers than Colt had thought.

Still stunned from the blow to his head, he was half carried, half dragged to a waiting van.

"Take care of him, Brother Elmer," he heard Zack say, the threat clear in the man's tone. Zack must have known that Brother Elmer was a weak link. "Brother Carl will go with you to make sure the job is done properly."

The van door slammed. Elmer started the engine and pulled away. The whole operation had taken less than ten minutes.

"DON'T HURT HIM!" Lola had cried as Colt was being dragged from the bedroom. Three women blocked her way to keep her from going after the men.

"Dress!" Sister Caroline ordered.

"My baby?"

"Grace will be safe as long as you do what we ask," Sister Amelia said. But there was something in Amelia's tone, a sadness that said not even she believed it.

Lola had no choice. They had Colt. They had Grace. She dressed quickly in a blouse and jeans, pulled on her sneakers and let the women lead her outside to a waiting van.

Sister Shelly was already in the van and holding Grace.

"Let me hold her," Lola said, steel in her voice.

The women looked at one another.

"Give the baby to Lola," Sister Amelia said and Shelly complied.

She sat holding the now-fussing Grace as the van pulled away. "Where are they taking Colt?"

No one answered. Her heart fell. Hadn't she feared that Jonas would retaliate? He'd be humiliated and would have to strike back. Isn't that what the sheriff had warned them about?

But what could he hope to achieve by this? The sheriff would know who took them. The first place Flint Cahill would look was the compound.

She remembered something she'd overheard while a prisoner at SLS. Some of the women had been worried that Jonas wasn't himself, that his memory seemed to be failing him. He often called them by the wrong names, got lost in the middle of a sermon. They questioned in hushed voices if it was his heart or something else, since they'd seem him taking pills for it.

"What is going on?" Lola asked, sensing something different about the group of women.

"We're leaving Montana," Sister Amelia said, and the other sisters tried to hush her. "She'll know soon enough," Amelia argued. "Father Jonas announced it earlier. He's selling the land here. Some are going to a new home in Arizona. Others…" Her voice broke. "I don't know where they're going."

Lola realized that their leader wasn't here. "Where is Sister Rebecca?" The question was met with silence. "Amelia?"

"She's gone."

"Everyone is leaving," Sister Shelly said, sounding near tears. "Father Jonas… He's letting Brother Zack lead the group in Arizona. He will be Father Zack now."

Lola couldn't believe what she was hearing as the van reached the highway and headed toward the compound. "He's putting Zack in charge?" She knew that the women in this van must feel the same way she did about Zack. "Did Jonas say what he is planning to do?"

Silence. Lola hugged Grace to her, her fear mounting with each passing mile as the van turned onto the road up to the mountain. Lola saw no other taillights ahead. No headlights behind them. Where had they taken Colt?

COLT COULDN'T SEE OUT, but he could tell that Elmer and Carl weren't taking him to the compound. He had a pretty good idea what their orders had been when Zack had told Elmer to take care of him.

He was furious with himself. He'd thought Jonas would have no choice but to give up. He should have known better. He should have taken more precautions. Against so many, he knew he and Lola hadn't stood a chance.

When they'd gone to the compound and rescued Grace, he'd thought this could be settled without bloodshed. It was why he hadn't taken a gun to the compound the first time that night. He didn't want to kill one of Jonas's sheep. They were just following orders, though blindly, true enough. But he hadn't wanted trouble with the law.

Now, though, he saw there was no way out

of this. Jonas had taken Lola and Grace. Nothing was going to stop him. He was going to end this once and for all no matter whom he had to kill.

Colt rolled to his side. They'd bound his wrists with plastic ties. He worked to slip his hands under him. If he could get a foot into the cuffs, he knew he could break free.

As he did, he watched the men in the front seat. Neither turned around to check on him. He got the feeling they didn't like being awakened in the middle of the night for this any more than Colt had. And now they had been ordered to kill someone. They had to be questioning Jonas and the SLS. He already knew that Brother Elmer had a weak spot for Lola and her baby.

He managed to get his hands past his butt. He lay on his back, catching his breath for a moment before he pushed himself up. Once he had his hands in front of him…

The van slowed. Elmer shifted down and turned onto a bumpy road that jarred every muscle in Colt's body. Colt caught a glimpse of something out the back window and realized where they were taking him. The old gravel pits outside of Gilt Edge. He caught the scent of the water through the partially opened windows up front. It was the perfect place to dump a body. Weighted down, there was a good chance the remains would never be found.

He felt his heart pound as he worked to free his wrists. The plastic restraints popped—but not louder than the rattle of the van on the rough road. Colt went to work on the ones binding his ankles.

As the van came to a stop, he resumed his original position, his hands behind him, feet together as he lay on his side facing the door.

Both men got out. He waited, wondering if either of them was armed or if the plan had been simply to drown him.

The van door opened noisily. "Can you get him out?" Elmer asked his companion.

Carl grunted but reached for him.

Colt swung his feet around and kicked the man in the chest, sending Carl sprawling in the dirt. He followed with a quick jab to Elmer's jaw. The older man stumbled and sat down hard on the ground.

So far, Colt hadn't seen a weapon, but as he jumped out, he saw Carl fumbling for something behind him. The man came up with a pistol. Right away, Colt saw that he wasn't comfortable using it. But that didn't mean that Carl wouldn't get lucky and blow Colt's head off.

He rushed around the back of the van to the driver's side. Grabbing open the door, he leaped in and started the van. As he threw the engine into Reverse, he saw Carl trying to get a clear shot. Elmer had stumbled to his feet and was blocking Carl's way—either accidentally or on purpose.

Colt didn't try to figure out which as he hit the gas. The van shot back. He cranked the wheel hard, swinging the back end toward the two men.

Carl got off two shots. One bullet shattered the back window of the van. The other took out Colt's side window, showering him with glass, and just missing his head before burying itself in the passenger-side door.

Elmer had parked the van close to the edge of the gravel pit, no doubt to make unloading his body easier.

As Colt swung the van at the two men, they tried to move out of the way. But Elmer was old and lost his footing. He was the first to go tumbling down the steep embankment and splash into the cold, clear water.

Carl had been busy trying to hit his target with the gun so he was caught unaware when the back of the van hit him and knocked him backward into the gravel pit. He let out a yell as he fell, the sound dying off in a loud splash.

Colt shifted into first gear and tore off down the bumpy road, thankful to be alive. He hoped both men could swim. If so, they had a long swim across the pit to where they would be able to climb out.

If either of their cell phones still worked after that, they might be able to warn Jonas. Not that it would matter.

Colt sped toward his house to get what he needed. This time he was taking weapons— and no prisoners.

FOR LOLA, WALKING into Jonas's cabin with the bundle in her arms felt a little like déjà vu. Only this time, there was a precious sleeping baby instead of rocks in her arms. As she entered, propelled by Brother Zack, she told herself that she would die protecting her daughter. Did Jonas know that, as well?

"Leave her," Jonas ordered. Zack started

to argue, but one look at their leader and he left, saying he would be right outside the door if he was needed. The sisters scattered, and the door closed, leaving Lola and Grace alone with Jonas.

He still had a bandage on the side of his head, but she knew better than to think his injury might slow him down.

"You are a very difficult woman."

"Only when someone tries to force me into doing something I don't want to do or they take my child from me."

He glanced at the bundle in her arms. "May I see her?"

Lola didn't move. "What do you hope to get out of this?" she demanded.

"I thought I was clear from the beginning. I want you. It's what your parents wanted—"

"I don't believe that. I heard from my father before he…died. He wanted out of SLS. He was trying to convince my mother to leave. I believe that's why you killed them both."

Jonas shook his head. "Are we back to that?"

"You're a fraud. This is no church. And you are no god. All this is only about your ego. It's a bad joke."

"Are you purposely trying to rile me?"

"I thought maybe it was time you heard the truth from someone instead of Sister Rebecca telling you how wonderful you are."

"Sister Rebecca is no longer with us."

"So I heard. Did you kill her yourself or make one of your sheep do it?" She knew he could not let Rebecca simply walk away. She'd been with him from the beginning. She'd done things for him, knew things.

"Why do you torment me? I cared about Rebecca."

"And yet you had her killed. I don't like the way you care about people."

At the sound of vehicles and activity on the mountain below them, Lola moved cautiously to the window, careful not to turn her back on Jonas.

She frowned as she saw everyone appearing to be packing up and moving. Fear coursed through her. "What's going on? I thought they weren't leaving until tomorrow?"

"Our time in Montana has come to an end. We are abandoning our church here."

What Amelia had told her was true. "So they're scurrying away like rats fleeing a sinking ship. You're really going to let them go?"

"All good things must end."

She thought of Colt as she had on the ride to the compound. Something told her that he hadn't been brought here. "Where is Colt?"

Jonas shook his head. "As I said, all good things must end."

Tears burned her eyes. "If you hurt him—"

'What will you do? Kill me? They will put you in prison, take away your baby. No, it is time you realized that you have never been in control. You are mine. You will always be mine. I will go to any lengths, including having Grace taken away so you never see her again if that's what it takes to keep you with me."

Fear turned her blood to ice as she looked into his eyes and understood he wasn't bluffing.

"You have only one choice. Come with me willingly and Grace will join us once we are settled."

No, she screamed silently. She didn't trust this man. But she also knew she couldn't keep someone like Zack from ripping Grace from her arms. Just as she knew that Jonas wasn't making an empty threat. She'd known this man was dangerous, but she hadn't realized how much he was willing to give up to have her—and Grace.

"You have only a few minutes to make up your mind, Lola." He had his phone in his hand. "Once I push this button, Zack will take Grace. If you ever want to see her again, you will agree to go with me."

"Where?" She knew she was stalling, fighting to find a way out of this. Colt. If he was dead, did she care what happened to her as long as she had his baby with her?

"Europe, South America. I haven't decided yet. Somewhere far away from all this. I have money. We will live well. We will be a family."

She thought of the family Colt had promised her and felt the ring on her finger.

Jonas's gaze went to her left hand. His face contorted in anger. "Take that off. Take that off now!"

Chapter Eighteen

Colt dialed the number quickly, knowing he had no choice even if he ended up behind bars. It would be worth it as long as Lola and Grace were safe from Jonas Emanuel once and for all.

"I need to borrow a helicopter," he said, the moment his friend answered.

"Mind if I ask what for?" Tommy Garrett asked, sounding like a man dragged from sleep in the wee hours of the morning. Tommy worked as a helicopter mechanic outside of Great Falls. Colt had served with him in Afghanistan and trusted the man with his life—and Lola's and Grace's.

"A madman has the woman I love and my baby daughter."

There was a beat of silence before Tommy said, "You planning to do this alone?"

"Better that way. I'll leave you out of it."

"Like hell. Tell me where you are. Outside my shop I have a Bell UH-1 Huey that needs its shakedown. The old workhorse is being used to fight forest fires. I'm on my way."

Colt knew the Huey could do up to 120 mph. But a safe cruising speed for helicopters was around a hundred. Without having to deal with traffic, road speeds or winding highways, the response time in a helicopter was considerably faster than anything on the ground. It was one reason Colt loved flying them.

So he wasn't surprised when Tommy landed in the pasture next to Colt's house thirty minutes later. The sun was coming up, chasing away the last of the dark. He could make out the mountains in the distance. Within a matter of minutes, they would be at the compound. He tried not think about what they would find.

"How much trouble is this going to get you in?" Colt asked his friend as he loaded the weapons in the back and climbed into the left seat, the crew chief seat.

"You just worry about what happens when we put this bird down," Tommy said in the adjacent seat at the controls.

As they headed for the mountaintop in the

distance, Colt told him everything that had happened from that moment in the hotel in Billings to earlier that night.

When he finished, Tommy said, "So this woman is the one?"

For a moment, Colt could only nod around the lump in this throat. "I've never met anyone like her."

"Apparently this cult leader hasn't, either. Tell me you have a plan." He swore when Colt didn't answer right away.

"There will be armed guards who are under the control of the cult leader, Jonas Emanuel. But we don't have time to sneak up on them. You don't have to land. Just get close enough to the ground that I can jump," Colt said as he began to strap on one of the weapons he'd brought. "Did I mention that these people are like zombies?"

"Great, you know how I love zombies. Except you can't kill zombies."

"These are religious zealots. I suspect they will be as hard to kill as zombies."

"This just keeps getting better and better," Tommy joked.

Colt looked over at him. "Thank you."

"Thank me after we get out with this woman

you've fallen in love with and your daughter." He shook his head. "You never did anything like normal people."

"No, I never did. There's the road that goes up to the compound."

Tommy swooped down, skimming just over the tops of the pines, and Colt saw something he hadn't expected.

"What the hell?" As they got closer to the mountain, Colt spotted the line of vans coming off the mountain. He felt a chill. "Something's going on. Fly closer to those vehicles," he said to Tommy, who immediately dipped down.

Inside the vans, he saw the faces of Jonas followers. There were a dozen vans. As each passed, he saw the pale faces, the fear in their eyes.

"Where do you think they're going?" Tommy asked.

"I have no idea. Leaving for good, from the looks of it. What is Jonas up to? Are these people decoys or are they really clearing out?" He thought of Lola and the baby. How crazy was Jonas? Would he kill them and then kill himself, determined that Colt would never have either of them?

"Up there," Colt said, pointing to the mountaintop. Tommy swung the helicopter in the direction he pointed. Within a few minutes, the buildings came into sight. Colt didn't see any guards. He didn't see anyone. The place looked deserted. Had everyone left?

Not everyone, he noticed. There was a large black SUV sitting in front of Jonas's cabin.

"Think you can put her into that clearing in front of the cabin?"

"Seriously?" Tommy said. "You forget who you're talking to. Give me a dime and I can set her down on it." Colt chuckled because he knew it was true.

LOLA LOOKED DOWN at the antique ring that Colt had put on her finger. She swore she would never take it off. It felt so right on her finger. Colt felt so right.

Jonas moved faster than she thought he could after his injury. He grabbed the baby from her arms and shoved her. She fell back, coming down hard on the floor. "I told you to take if off. Now!"

"Give me Grace."

"Her name is Angel, and if you don't do what I say this moment…"

Lola pulled off the ring. She knew it was silly. Colt was probably dead. She'd lost so much. What did a ring matter at this point? The one thing she couldn't lose was Grace, and yet she felt as if she already had in more ways than one. Jonas had them captive. He could do whatever he wanted with Grace. Just as he could do whatever he wanted with her now.

"Happy?" she asked, still clutching the ring in her fist.

"Throw it away." He pointed toward the fireplace and the cold ashes filling it.

She hesitated again.

"Do as I say!" Jonas bellowed at her, waking up Grace. The baby began to cry.

Lola tossed the ring toward the fireplace. It was a lazy, bad throw, one that made Jonas's already furious face cloud over even more. The ring missed the fireplace opening, pinged off the rock and rolled under the couch. She looked at Jonas. If he really did have a bad heart, she realized his agitation right now could kill him. She doubted she would get that lucky, though.

He seemed to be trying to calm down.

Grace kept crying and she could tell it was getting on his nerves.

She got to her feet. "Let me have her. She'll quit crying for me."

He shook his head. "I'm not sure I can trust you," he said slowly.

Colt was gone. The ring was gone. But Jonas had something much more precious. He had Grace. But Lola wasn't giving up.

"How do I know I can trust *you*?" she said.

The question surprised him. He'd expected her to cower, to promise him anything. She knew better than to do that. Jonas was surrounded by people who bowed down to him. Lola never had and maybe that's why he was so determined to have her.

She approached him. "You hurt my baby and I will kill you. I'll cut your throat in your sleep. Or push you down a flight of stairs. Or poison your food. It might take me a while to get the opportunity, but believe me, I will do it."

He chuckled as his gaze met hers. "I do believe you. I've always loved your spirit. Your mother told me what a headstrong young woman you were. She wasn't wrong."

It hurt to have him mention her mother. Was

it possible that Jonas could get away with the murders he'd committed? She feared it was. She thought of Colt and felt a sob rise in her throat. She forced it back down. She couldn't show weakness, not now, especially not for Colt. She had to think about Grace.

"We seem to be at an impasse," Jonas said. "What do you suggest we do?"

"I suggest you give me my baby and let me leave here."

He shook his head. "Not happening. Neither you or your baby will be leaving here— except with me."

"So what are you waiting for?" she demanded.

Jonas chuckled as he tilted his head as if to listen. "We're waiting for Colt. I just have a feeling he will somehow manage to try to save you one more time."

Lola listened as her heart thumped against her rib cage. Colt? He was alive? She thought she heard what sounded like a helicopter headed this way.

"I believe that's him now."

COLT FOUGHT THE bad feeling that had settled in the pit of his stomach. Jonas was playing hardball this time. He wasn't going to let Lola and Grace go—not without a fight to the death. That's if they were still alive.

"Change of plans," he said to Tommy. He felt as if time was running out for Lola and Grace. "Put us down and wait for me," he said, fear making his voice sound strained as he passed Tommy a handgun. "I hope you won't have to use this. It appears that the guards have left, but I've already underestimated Jonas once and I don't want to do it again. I'm hoping this won't take long."

As Colt started to jump out, Tommy grabbed his sleeve. "Be careful."

Colt nodded. "You, too."

"I'll be here. Good luck."

Colt knew that if there was anyone he wanted on his side in a war it was Tommy Garrett—and this was war. These soldiers would die for their leader. They were just as devoted to dying for their cause as the ones he'd fought in Afghanistan.

The moment the chopper touched the ground, he leaped out and ran up the mountainside to where a large black SUV sat, the engine running and Brother Zack behind the wheel. Behind him, he heard Tommy shut down the engine. The rotors began to slow.

Colt looked around. The only person he'd seen so far was Zack, but that didn't mean that another of the guards hadn't stayed behind.

As he approached the SUV, he could hear the bass coming from the stereo. Closer, he saw that Zack had on headphones and was rockin' out. He must have had the stereo cranked, which explained why he hadn't heard the helicopter land. Nor had he heard him approach.

Colt yanked open the door. A surprised Zack turned. Colt grabbed him by his shirt and hauled him out. Unfortunately, Zack was carrying and he went for his gun. Zack was strong and combat trained. But Colt was fighting for Lola's and Grace's lives.

Colt managed to get hold of the man's arm, twisting it to the point of snapping as they struggled for the weapon. When the shot went off, it was muffled—just like Zack's grunt. Blood blossomed on the front of Zack's white shirt. The gun dropped, falling under the SUV.

As the man slumped, Colt shoved him back inside the vehicle, shut off the stereo and slammed the door before turning to Jonas's cabin. He'd seen suitcases in the back of the SUV and suspected the sheep weren't the only ones fleeing.

Colt pulled his holstered gun and climbed the steps. He had another gun stuck in the back of his jeans under his jacket. He always liked to be prepared—especially against someone like Jonas Emanuel.

He could still hear the sweep of the helicopter's rotors as they continued to slow. The wooden porch floor creaked under his boots. He braced himself and reached for the doorknob.

Before he could turn it, Lola opened the door. Her face had lost all its color. Her violet eyes appeared huge. He could see that she'd been crying. The sight froze him in place for moment. What had Jonas done to her? To Grace?

"Where is Jonas?" Colt asked quietly. Suddenly there wasn't a sound, not even a meadowlark from the grass or a breeze moaning in the pines. The eerie quiet sent a chill up his spine. "Lola?" The word came in a whisper.

"I'm leaving with Jonas," she said.

"Like hell." He could see that Jonas had

put the fear into her and used Grace to do it. He'd never wanted to strangle anyone with his bare hands more than he did the cult leader at this moment.

"Please, it's what I want." Her words said one thing; her blue eyes pleaded with him to save Grace.

He pushed past her to find Jonas sitting in a chair just yards away. He was holding Grace in such a way that it stopped Colt cold.

JONAS RELISHED THE expression on Colt's handsome face. It almost made everything worth what he was going to have to give up. The cowboy thought he could just bust in here and take Lola and the baby? Not this time.

"Lola is going with me and so is her baby," he said as he turned the baby so she was facing her biological father and dangling from his fingers. He wanted Colt to see the baby's face and realize what he would be risking if he didn't back off.

"I don't think so," Colt said, but without much conviction. Jonas was ready to throw the baby against the rock fireplace if Colt took another step. The cowboy wasn't stupid. He'd figured that out right away. But he'd been stupid enough to come up here again. The man should have been dead.

Idly, Jonas wondered what had gone wrong at the gravel pit. He'd known he couldn't depend on Elmer, but he was disposable. Brother Carl had inspired more faith that he would get the job done. Jonas had assumed that Carl would have to kill both Elmer and Colt. Clearly, the job had been too much for him.

"Has he hurt you?" Colt asked Lola.

She shook her head.

Jonas was touched by the cowboy's concern, but quickly getting bored with all this. "Elmer and Carl?" he asked, curious.

"Swimming, that is, if either of them knows how," Colt answered.

"And Brother Zack?"

"No longer listening to music in your big SUV."

So he couldn't depend on Zack to come to his rescue. Another surprise. Everyone was letting him down. Just as well that he was packing it all in. He'd grown tired of the squabbling among the sisters and the back-biting of the brothers. Human nature really was malicious.

Still, he would miss Zack. And now who

would lead his people to the promised land of Arizona? He chuckled to himself since he didn't own any land in Arizona. But they wouldn't know that until they got there, would they?

He saw the cowboy shoot a look at Lola. She was standing off to Colt's left as if she didn't know what to do. He could see the tension in her face. She wasn't being so smart-mouthed now, was she? As much as he was enjoying this, he didn't have to ask what she was hoping would happen here.

But, this time, she'd been outplayed. The cowboy was going to lose. It was simply a matter of how much he would have to lose before this was over. Did he realize that he wasn't getting out of here alive? At this point, Jonas wasn't sure he cared if Lola and the baby survived either, though he still wanted the woman, and damned if he wouldn't have her—dead or alive. The thought didn't even surprise him. His father used to say that one day he would reach rock bottom. Was this it?

"Why would you want a woman who doesn't love you?" Colt asked conversationally, as if they were old friends discussing the weather—and took a step closer.

"Because I can have her. I can have anything I want, and I want her. The baby is optional. I guess that's up to you."

"How's that?"

"You can't reach me before I hurl your baby into the rock fireplace. But if you try, I will, and then we will only be talking about Lola. The thing is, I don't think she will love you anymore, not after you got her baby killed," Jonas said. "Want to take a chance on that? Take another step…"

COLT COULD SEE that Jonas's arms were tiring from holding Grace up the way he was. He was using the baby like a shield. There was no way Colt could get a shot off with Jonas sitting and the baby out in front of him. Nor could he chance that, as he fired, Jonas wouldn't throw Grace into the rocks.

One glance at Lola and he knew that what they both feared was a real possibility—Jonas could drop the baby at any moment. Or, worse, throw Grace against the rock fireplace as he was threatening.

"Colt, I'll go with him. It's the only way," Lola pleaded as she stepped to him, grabbing his arm.

It was a strange thing for her to do and for a moment he didn't understand. Then he felt her reach behind him to the pistol he had at his back. She must have seen the bulk of it under his shirt. She freed the gun and dropped her hands to her sides, keeping turned so Jonas couldn't see what she held. Then she began to cry.

"You heard her," Jonas said. "Leave before someone gets hurt. Before you get hurt." His arms were shaking visibly. "If you care anything about this child…"

Jonas knew Colt wasn't leaving without Lola and Grace. Saying he could walk away was all bluff. Did he have a weapon handy? Colt suspected so.

Lola was still halfway facing him so she could keep the gun in her hand hidden. Colt feared what she planned to do, but he could feel time running out. Jonas was losing patience. Worse, his arms were shaking now. He couldn't hold the baby much longer—and he couldn't back down. Wouldn't.

"Tell him, Jonas," she cried, suddenly running toward the cult leader and dropping to her knees only feet from him after sticking the gun in the waist of her jeans. "Tell him I'm going with you, and that it's true and to leave."

The cult leader hadn't expected her to do that. For a moment, it looked as if he was going to throw the baby. Before he could, Lola grabbed for Grace with her left hand. At the same time, she pulled the pistol from behind her with her right. She had hold of Grace's chubby little leg and wasn't letting go.

Everything happened fast after that. Colt, seeing what Lola had planned, took the shot the moment Lola managed to pull the baby down and away from Jonas's smug face. Colt had always been an expert shot. Even during the most stressful situations.

He missed. Jonas had fallen forward just enough that the shot went over his head and lodged in the back of the chair. Before he could fire again, he heard Lola fire. She'd taken the shot from the floor, shooting under Grace to hit the man low in the stomach. He saw Jonas release Grace as he grabbed for his bleeding belly.

Lola dropped the gun and pulled Grace into her arms. They were both crying. As Colt rushed to the cult leader, his gun leveled at the man's head, Lola scrambled away from Jonas with Grace tucked in her arms.

Jonas was holding his stomach with one hand and fumbling for something in the chair with the other. Colt was aiming to shoot, to finish Jonas, when he saw that it wasn't a gun the cult leader was going for. It was the man's phone.

He watched Jonas punch at the screen, his bloody fingers slippery, his hands shaking. It took a moment for the alert to sound. Jonas seemed to wait, one bloody hand on his stomach, the other on his phone. He stared at the front door, expecting it to come flying open as one of the guards burst in.

Seconds passed, then several minutes. Nothing happened. Jonas looked wild-eyed at the door as if he couldn't believe it.

"They've all left," Colt said. "There is no one to help you."

Jonas looked down at his phone. With trembling fingers he made several attempts to key in 9-1-1 and finally gave up. "You have to call an ambulance. It's the humane thing to do."

"This from the man who was about to kill my baby daughter?"

"You would let me bleed to death?"

Colt looked over at Lola, huddled in the corner with Grace. Their gazes met. He pulled out his own phone and keyed in 9-1-1. He asked to speak to the sheriff.

When he was connected with Flint, he said, "You were right. Jonas hit us in the middle of the night. He sent two men to kill me. I left them in the old gravel pits. He took Lola and Grace, but they are both safe now. Unfortunately, one of his guards tried to shoot me. He's dead outside here on the compound and Jonas is wounded, so you'll need an ambulance and a—" He was going to say *coroner*, but before he could get the word out, the front door of the cabin banged open.

He spun around in time to see Zack bleeding and barely able to stand, but the man could still shoot. He fired the weapon in his hand in a barrage of bullets before Colt could pull the trigger.

LOLA SCREAMED. GRACE WAILED. It happened so fast. She'd thought it was all over. Finally. She'd thought they were finally safe. And so had Colt. He hadn't expected Zack to be alive—let alone come in shooting—any more than she had.

Colt threw himself in Grace's and her direction. As he did, he brought up the weapon he'd been holding on Jonas. The air filled with the loud reports of gunfire.

Lola laid her body over Grace's to protect her, knowing that Colt had thrown himself toward them to do the same. It took her a few moments to realize that the firing had stopped. She peeked out, terrified that she would find Colt lying dead at her feet.

Colt lay on his side, his back to her. She put Grace down long enough to reach for him. He was holding his leg, blood oozing out from between his fingers. He looked up at her.

"Are you and Grace—"

"We're fine. But you're bleeding," Lola cried.

"It's just a flesh wound," Colt said. "Don't worry about me. As long as you and Grace are all right…" He grimaced as he tried to get to his feet.

In the doorway, Zack lay crumpled on the floor. Lola couldn't tell if he was breathing or not. Her gaze swung to Jonas. He had tumbled out of his chair. He wasn't breathing, given that the top of his head was missing. She looked away quickly.

Grace's wailing was the only sound in the room. She rushed to her. As she did, she saw Colt's cell phone on the floor and picked it up. The sheriff was still there.

"We need an ambulance. Colt is wounded. Zack and Jonas are dead."

"Tommy," Colt said, trying to get to his feet. "He would have seen Zack heading for the cabin…" He limped to the door and pushed it open. Beyond it, he saw Tommy slumped over the controls of the helicopter. "There isn't time to wait for an ambulance. Tell the sheriff we'll be at the hospital."

As she related to the sheriff what Colt had said, she hurried to the couch. Squatting down, she fished her ring from under it. Her gentle toss of it hadn't hurt the ring or the diamonds. She slipped it on her finger, feeling as if now she could face anything again. Then, holding Grace in her arms, she ran after Colt to the helicopter sitting like a big dark bird in the middle of the compound.

COLT IGNORED THE pain as he ran to the helicopter. When he reached Tommy, he hurriedly felt for a pulse. For a moment, he thought his friend was dead, and yet he didn't see any blood. He found a pulse and felt a wave of relief. He'd dragged his friend into this. The last thing he wanted to do was get him killed.

On closer inspection, he could see a bump the size of a goose egg on Tommy's head. He figured Zack must have ambushed him before coming up to the cabin to finish things.

"Is he…?" Lola asked from behind him. She held a crying Grace in her arms and was trying to soothe her.

"He's alive, but we need to get him to the hospital. Come around the other side and climb in the back with Grace." Colt helped them in and then slid into the seat and took over the controls. He started up the motor. The rotors began to turn and then spin. A few minutes later, he lifted off and headed for Gilt Edge.

The helicopter swept over the tops of the pines and out of the mountains. Colt glanced over at Tommy. He seemed to be coming around. In the back, Lola had calmed Grace down and she now slept in her mother's arms.

He told himself that all was right with the world. Lola and Grace were safe. Tommy was going to make it. But he was feeling the effects of his blood loss as he saw the hospital's helipad in the distance. He'd never lost a bird. He told himself he wasn't going to lose this one—especially with the precious cargo he was carrying.

Colt set the chopper down and turned off the engine. After that, everything became a blur. He knew he'd lost a lot of blood and was light-headed, but it wasn't until he'd shut down the chopper and tried to get out that he realized how weak he was.

The last thing he remembered was seeing hospital staff rushing toward the helicopter pushing two gurneys.

Chapter Nineteen

Colt woke to find Lola and Grace beside his bed. He tried to sit up, but Lola gently pushed him back down.

"Tommy is fine," she told him as if knowing exactly what he needed to hear. "A mild concussion. The doctor is having a terrible time keeping him in bed. We're all fine now."

Colt relaxed back on the pillows and smiled. "I was so worried. But everyone's all right?"

She nodded. "I was worried about you." She pushed a lock of hair back from his forehead and looked into his eyes. "You lost so much blood, but the doctor says you're going to be fine."

He glanced over at the IV attached to his arm. "I remember flying the chopper to the hospital but not much after that." He took her hand and squeezed it. "How is Grace?"

"Sleeping." Lola pointed to the bassinet the nurses had brought in for her. "I refused to leave until I knew you were all right." They'd also brought in a cot for Lola, he saw. "I've just been going back and forth from your room to Tommy's."

Colt smiled, took her hand and squeezed it. "I almost lost you. Again."

"But you saved me. Again. Aren't you getting tired of it?"

He shook his head. "Never." He glanced down at the ring on her finger. When he'd come into the cabin, he'd seen her rubbing the spot on her left hand where it had been. He hadn't been surprised Jonas hadn't liked seeing the ring on her finger. "When are you going to marry me?"

"You name the day. But right now you're in the middle of selling your ranch and holding an auction, and the doctor isn't going to let you out of here for a while. The bullet missed bone, but your leg is going to take some time to heal. Also, I believe you missed your appointment with your Realtor."

Colt grimaced. "Margaret. She is going to be furious."

"I called her. Apparently, ending up in the hospital bought you some time."

"I need to talk to Tommy, but I want to talk to him about my plan for the future, for *our* future."

The hospital-room door opened and Sheriff Flint Cahill stuck his head in. "Our patient awake? I hate to interrupt, but I need to talk to Colt if he's up to it."

Colt pulled Lola down for a kiss. "I'll talk to the sheriff. You can leave Grace. If she wakes up, I'll take care of her."

She nodded. "I know you will." She said hello to the sheriff. "I'll just be down the hall."

Flint took off his Stetson and pulled up a chair. "I've already spoken with Tom Garrett and Lola. I have their statements, but I need yours. I have two dead men up on the mountain, two suffering from dehydration and two more in the hospital. Elmer and Carl have been picked up. They both said they were the ones who almost got killed, not you." He pulled out his notebook and pen. "Said you knocked them into the gravel pit."

Colt nodded. "After they took me from my house in the middle of the night, tied me up and planned to kill me and dump me in the pit. They probably didn't mention that."

"Actually, Elmer confessed this morning. They're both behind bars." The sheriff sighed. "Just give me the basics. You'll have to come down to the office when you're released."

Colt related everything from the time he was awakened by the cult members breaking into the house until he landed the helicopter at the hospital.

"It would have been nice if you'd given me a call," Flint said.

"Jonas would have killed them. He was so close to hurting Grace…" His voice broke. "If Lola hadn't acted when she did…"

"Jonas had one bullet in him from a gun registered to you, but all the others were from a gun registered to Jonas himself. We found it next to Zack's body. Why would Zack kill his own leader?"

Colt shook his head. "He came in firing. When I jumped out of the way, he kept firing…"

"He's the one who wounded you?"

"Yes. And the one who knocked out Tommy, but he might have already told you that."

"Actually," the sheriff said. "He didn't see who or what hit him."

"Zack was the only guard left. Everyone else vacated the property."

"Lola said that most of them were headed to Arizona, where Jonas had promised them a place to live, but we can't find any property owned by him or SLS," Flint said. "We did, though, find a variety of places where he has stashed their money, a lot of it. I would imagine there'll be lawsuits against his estate."

"Lola thinks he murdered her parents. They're buried on the compound."

The sheriff raked a hand through his hair. "We saw that there is a new grave in the woods. We were able to contact a couple of SLS followers who didn't make it any farther than town. They said they think he killed Sister Rebecca and that she is buried in the new grave." He shook his head. "He had me fooled."

"Me, too. For a while," Colt admitted.

Grace began to whimper next to his bed.

The sheriff put away his notebook and pen as he rose. "I'll let you see to your daughter." He tipped his Stetson as he left.

THE STORY HIT the local paper the next day. SLS members were spilling their guts about what had gone on up at the compound. A half dozen had already filed lawsuits against the fortune Jonas had amassed.

The article made Colt and Tommy sound like heroes. Colt figured that was Lola's doing since she'd told him she'd been interviewed by a reporter. She'd said she was anxious for her story—and that of her parents—to get out.

"Maybe it will keep other people from getting taken in by men like Jonas," she'd said. "He caught my parents at a vulnerable time in their lives. But if they could be fooled, then anyone can."

Lola picked him up after the doctor released him from the hospital.

He sat in the passenger seat of the SUV she'd had delivered to his house. The woman was damned independent, but he liked that about her. Grace grinned at him from the car seat as they drove out to the ranch. Drove home. Well, home for a while anyway. All he'd been able to think about was getting back to that old ranch house that had felt like a prison before Lola. Now it felt like home.

Not that he was going to get sentimental and hang on to the house. Or the ranch. He wanted a new start for his little family.

They'd been home for a while when Tommy stopped by the house to see how he was doing before taking his helicopter home.

"You've met Lola," Colt said.

Tommy nodded.

"We got to know each other while we were waiting on you to get well. I had to thank him for all he did in helping us." She turned to the man from where she was making cookies in the kitchen. "We owe you. If you can stick around for twelve minutes, I will have a batch of chocolate chip cookies coming out of the oven. It's not much, given what you did for us."

"I'm just glad you're all right," Tommy said, looking bashful. "Anyway, I owe your husband. He saved my life. I'd do anything for him. I got to tell you, I think our boy Colt has done good this time," his friend said, grinning at Lola, then Colt. "You got yourself a good one," he said with a wink. "So what's this plan you wanted to talk to me about?"

"You're not mad at me for almost getting you killed?" Colt asked.

Tommy looked embarrassed. "I let some cult member sneak up on me."

"Zack was ex-military."

"That makes me feel a little better, but let's keep it to ourselves, okay? So what's up?" he asked as he took the chair he was offered at the kitchen table. Lola checked the cookies. Grace was watching her from her carrier on the counter. Colt liked watching Lola cook. He just liked watching her and marveling at how lucky he'd gotten.

"Colt?" Tommy said, grinning as he drew his attention again.

He laughed, then got serious. "Remember all the times we talked about starting our own helicopter service?" Colt and Tommy had spent hours at night in Afghanistan planning what they would do when they got out of the Army. Only Colt had stayed in, so their dream of owning their own flight company had been put off indefinitely.

"You still thinking about it?" Tommy asked.

"I know you're doing great with your repair business. I know you might not be interested in starting a company with me, but I've sold the ranch. I have money to invest. You don't have to answer right now. Take a few days to—"

"I don't need a few days. Absolutely," his friend said. "Where were you thinking of headquartering it?"

"There's a piece of land close by I'd like to build a house on. Right down the road from it would be the ideal place for the office, with lots of room for the shops and landing any number of birds."

Tommy laughed. "You really have been thinking about this." He glanced past Colt to Lola, who was busy taking the cookies out of the oven. "What about the military?" he asked, his gaze shifting back to Colt.

"I've decided not to take the upcoming assignment and resign my commission. I'm getting married. I have a family now. I don't want to be away from them."

"I get it," Tommy said as he took the warm cookie Lola offered him. "How soon?"

"I can make an offer on the land and we can get construction going on the shops and hangers—"

"How long before you get married?" Tommy asked with a laugh and took a bite of the cookie, before complimenting Lola.

"In three weeks. That was something else I needed to talk to you about," Colt said. "I need a best man."

LOLA WANTED TO pinch herself. She couldn't believe she was getting married. She'd never been so happy. She was glad they'd put off the wedding for a few weeks. There'd been a lot of questions about everything that had happened up on the mountain. The investigation, though, had finally ended.

It had taken a while for the bodies of her parents and Sister Rebecca to be exhumed. Just as she'd suspected, autopsies revealed that both of her parents had been poisoned. So had Rebecca. Lola made arrangements to have their remains flown to California and reinterred in the plots next to her sister's.

"You have nothing to feel guilty about," Colt had assured her.

"But if I'd come straight home after university and tried to get them out of that place—"

"You know it wouldn't have done any good. They were determined that you join them, right?"

She'd nodded. "But if I'd come right home

when I got my father's letter, maybe I could have—"

"You know how Jonas operated. It wouldn't have made a difference. You said yourself that your mother adored Jonas. You couldn't have gotten her to leave and your father wouldn't have left without her, right?"

She'd known he was right. Still, she hated that she hadn't been able to save them. She was just grateful to Colt. If it hadn't been for him...

Lola looked down at her sleeping daughter. Yes, if it hadn't been for him there would have been no Grace.

COLT WANDERED THROUGH the days afterward, more content than he had ever been. He and Lola went horseback riding. She took to it so well that she made him promise he would teach Grace when she was old enough.

"I'll teach all of the kids."

"All of the kids?" she'd asked with one raised eyebrow.

He'd smiled as he'd pulled her to him. "Tell me you wouldn't mind having a couple more."

"You want a son."

"I want whatever you give me," he'd said,

nuzzling her neck and making her laugh. "I'll be taking all girls if that's what you've got for me."

Lola had kissed him, promising to give him as many children as he wanted.

"And I'll teach them all to fly. Which reminds me, anytime you want to go for a ride… The helicopters will be coming in right after the wedding."

The new owners of the ranch had allowed Colt to stay on with his family until he was able to get a mobile home put on the land he'd bought back from them. "We'll live in it until the house is finished, then maybe use it for the office until the office building is done."

Lola seemed as excited as he was about the business they were starting with Tommy. She kept busy with her new friends Lillie and Mariah. They were actually talking playdates for the kids.

He ran into Wyatt a couple more times in town. He hadn't wanted to slug him. Actually, he'd wanted to thank him. The thought had made him laugh.

Also, Colt hadn't been that surprised when Julia called. He almost hadn't answered. "Hello?"

"Colt, it's Julia. I saw your engagement announcement in the newspaper not long after that story came out. What a story."

He didn't know what to say.

"Wyatt and I are over. I know you don't care, but I wanted you to hear it from me first."

"I'm sorry." He really was. He no longer had any ill will toward either of them and said as much.

"I won't bother you again. I'm actually leaving town. But I had to ask you something…" She seemed to hesitate. "It's amazing what you did for this Lola woman. You really put up a fight to save her and the baby."

He waited, wondering where she was going with this.

"Why…" Her voice broke. "Why didn't you put up a fight for me?"

It had never crossed his mind to try to keep Julia from marrying Wyatt. She was right. He hadn't put up a fight. He'd been hurt, he'd been angry, but he hadn't made some grandiose effort like riding a horse into the church to stop the wedding—if it had ever gone that far.

"I hope you find what you're looking for,"

he said, because there wasn't anything else he could say.

"And I hope you're unhappy as hell." She disconnected.

He looked over at Lola and laughed.

"Julia," she said.

"Yep, she called to say she liked the article." Lola smiled. "You're a terrible liar."

"She's leaving town."

"Really?" She didn't seem unhappy to hear that.

"She wished us well."

"Now I know you're lying," she said as he pulled her close.

THE WEDDING TOOK PLACE in a field of flowers surrounded by the four mountain ranges. Colt had purchased the property just days before. He'd had to scramble to get everything moved in for the ceremony.

What had started as a small wedding had grown, as old and new friends wanted to be a part of it.

"Lola, I know this isn't what we planned," Colt had apologized. They'd agreed to a small wedding, and somehow it had gone awry.

She had laughed. "I love that all these

people care about you and want to be there. They're becoming my friends, as well." Lillie and Mariah had given her a baby shower, the three becoming instant friends.

He kissed her. "I just want it to be the best day of your life."

"That day was when I met you."

Colt couldn't believe how many people had helped to make the day special. Calls came in from around the world from men he'd served with. A dozen of them flew in for the ceremony. The guest list had continued to grow right up until the wedding.

"Let us cater it for you," Lillie and Mariah had suggested. "Darby insists. And the Stagecoach Saloon is all yours for the reception, if it rains."

Lola had hugged her new friends, eyes glistening and Colt thought he couldn't be more blessed. Lola had accepted their kind offer and added, "Only if the two of you will agree to be my matrons of honor."

So much had been going on that the weeks leading up to the wedding had flown by. Colt wished his father was alive to see this—his only son changing diapers, getting up for middle-of-the-night feedings, bathing the baby in the kitchen sink, and all the while loving every minute of it.

Tommy always chuckled when he came by and caught Colt being a father. "If the guys could see you now," he'd joked. But Colt had seen his friend's wistful looks. He hoped Tommy found someone he could love as much as Colt loved Lola.

She'd continued to amaze him, taking everything in her stride as the ranch auction was held and the sale of the ranch continued. She'd had her things shipped from where they'd been in storage and helped him start packing up what he planned to keep at the house.

He'd felt overwhelmed sometimes, but Lola was always cool and calm. He often thought of that woman he'd met in Billings—and the one he'd found on his doorstep in the middle of the night. Often he didn't feel he was good enough for her. But then she would find him, put her arms around him and rest her head on his shoulder, and he would breathe in the scent of her and know that this was meant to be.

Like standing here now in a field of flowers next to Lola with all their friends and the preacher ready to marry them. If this was a dream, he didn't want to wake up.

LOLA COULDN'T BELIEVE all the people who had come into her life because of Colt. She looked over at him. He was so handsome in his Western suit and boots. He was looking at her, his blue eyes shining. He smiled as the preacher said, "Do you take this woman—"

"I sure do," he said, and everyone laughed.

Lola hardly remembered the rest of the ceremony. She felt so blissfully happy that she wasn't even sure her feet had touched the ground all day.

But she remembered the kiss. Colt had pulled her to him, taking his time as he looked into her eyes. "I love you, Lola," he'd whispered.

She'd nodded through her tears and then he'd kissed her. The crowd had broken into applause. Cowboy hats and Army caps had been thrown into the air. Somewhere beyond the crowd, a band began to play.

Lillie hugged her before handing her Grace. Lola looked up from the infant she held in her arms, her eyes full of tears. Colt put his arm around both of them as they took their first steps as Mr. and Mrs. Colt McCloud.

* * * * *

Get 4 FREE REWARDS!

We'll send you 2 FREE Books plus 2 FREE Mystery Gifts.

Harlequin® Romantic Suspense books feature heart-racing sensuality and the promise of a sweeping romance set against the backdrop of suspense.

FREE Value Over **$20**

Get 4 FREE REWARDS!

We'll send you 2 FREE Books plus 2 FREE Mystery Gifts.

Harlequin Presents® books feature a sensational and sophisticated world of international romance where sinfully tempting heroes ignite passion.

FREE Value Over **$20**

YES! Please send me 2 FREE Harlequin Presents® novels and my 2 FREE gifts (gifts are worth about $10 retail). After receiving them, if I don't wish to receive any more books, I can return the shipping statement marked "cancel." If I don't cancel, I will receive 6 brand-new novels every month and be billed just $4.55 each for the regular-print edition or $5.55 each for the larger-print edition in the U.S., or $5.49 each for the regular-print edition or $5.99 each for the larger-print edition in Canada. That's a savings of at least 11% off the cover price! It's quite a bargain! Shipping and handling is just 50¢ per book in the U.S. and 75¢ per book in Canada*. I understand that accepting the 2 free books and gifts places me under no obligation to buy anything. I can always return a shipment and cancel at any time. The free books and gifts are mine to keep no matter what I decide.

Choose one: ☐ **Harlequin Presents®**
Regular-Print
(106/306 HDN GMYX)

☐ **Harlequin Presents®**
Larger-Print
(176/376 HDN GMYX)

HP18

Name (please print)

Address   Apt. #

City   State/Province   Zip/Postal Code

Mail to the **Reader Service:**
IN U.S.A.: P.O. Box 1341, Buffalo, NY 14240-8531
IN CANADA: P.O. Box 603, Fort Erie, Ontario L2A 5X3

Want to try two free books from another series? Call 1-800-873-8635 or visit www.ReaderService.com.

Get 2 Free Books,
Plus 2 Free Gifts—
just for trying the Reader Service!

WORLDWIDE LIBRARY®

WWL17R2